Afterall Our Love Story

By
Patty Bayman

TABLE OF CONTENTS

Dedication

To the love of my life, Brian. I will always love you. You swept me off my feet, and I still want to shout from the rooftops and tell the world how much I love you. The love we shared will last beyond our lifetime.

To my little Zoe, I miss you more than words can express. You, my precious sixteen-pound furry baby, were truly a blessing from above. You filled our lives with laughter and love.

Without the two of you, I feel entirely lost.

Preface

At just 18 years old, Patty met the love of her life. Brian, a jazz band instructor at her hometown college, was a handsome, kind-hearted, and gifted saxophonist. The two fell deeply in love, envisioning a long and happy life together. They had no way of knowing the challenges that would soon test their bond.

After their wedding, Brian and Patty moved to Bordeaux, France, where Brian earned a prestigious opportunity to study music under a renowned classical saxophonist. Their time in France was idyllic, as they embraced the culture, made lifelong friends, and cherished their life together. But their dream was suddenly shattered when Brian was hospitalized with a devastating case of encephalitis.

In the wake of his illness, Patty watched her vibrant, talented husband transform into someone entirely dependent, unable to walk or speak. Heartbroken but unwavering, Patty chose love over despair. Upon returning to the U.S., she dedicated herself to caring for Brian, devoting every day for 16 years to his well-being until his passing.

With a selfless love born of incredible strength, Patty fed, bathed, and comforted Brian, providing him with the dignity and devotion he deserved. *Afterall* is a tender and candid memoir that shares Patty's journey of heartbreak, resilience, and unwavering hope in the face of unimaginable adversity. More than just a story of struggle, it is a testament to the boundless power of the human spirit and the profound beauty of true love.

Chapter One
The August Day Everything Changed

W hen I was 18, I spent the summer in New York with my sister Susan. We left the day after my high school graduation, and I was eager to escape our small town. I didn't know what I wanted to do with my life, but I knew I needed a change.

Susan stayed with our aunt, and I worked as a nanny for our cousin's family in Mamaroneck. It was a summer filled with adventure and discovery. Susan and I explored New York City as much as we could, soaking in the sights, sounds, and energy of the city. We even took a trip to Washington, D.C., making memories I'll always cherish. It was exciting and everything I thought my hometown wasn't, but as the summer wore on, I began to realize something surprising: city life wasn't for me. I missed the wide-open spaces, stunning sunsets, and peaceful country roads I'd grown up with. While I enjoyed the buzz of the city, it didn't feel like home.

As the fall approached, I spent a lot of time thinking about my next steps. Staying in Mamaroneck seemed like a great option, and I had been offered the chance to continue working as a nanny and attend a local community college. On paper, it made sense. But deep down, I knew I wasn't ready for that kind of responsibility. Being a nanny felt too much like being a mom, and I realized I needed to figure out my own path before taking on the care of others.

1

Susan was returning home for her junior year of college, and something inside me told me I needed to go back, too. Just a few months earlier, I couldn't wait to leave that "Podunk" little town. But now, I felt it calling me back. I promised myself that I would use my freshman year to reflect and figure out what I truly wanted. Sometimes, the best way to move forward is to return to where you started. Trusting my instincts, I went home, ready to embrace the journey ahead.

Chadron, Nebraska, lies in the northwestern panhandle, just below the South Dakota border and nestled near the Pine Ridge Forest, where the air is crisp and clean. In 1977, my parents moved there from a small suburb outside Chicago, Illinois. My dad, an engineer for the railroad, sought a simpler life away from the hustle and humidity of the city, while my mom, the heart and soul of our family, created a warm and loving home wherever we went. Together, they brought their dream to life on 7 acres of land south of town, behind the college on what we called Mitchell's Mountain. Though it was more of a big hill than a true mountain, it became our sanctuary. Surrounded by ponderosa pines and sweeping countryside, they designed and built a home like no other. Nestled into the side of the hill, the east side of the house was shielded by a 12-foot embankment, while the west side featured floor-to-ceiling windows that opened up to breathtaking views of the valley and endless horizon. Though our home had all the modern amenities, it was built with sustainability in mind. We relied on a small wood-burning stove for heat and used passive solar energy from the sun streaming through the west-facing windows. Every board, brick, and beam bore my dad's touch; he built nearly the entire house by himself.

As a family, we worked together to landscape the property, creating winding footpaths that led to hidden spots perfect for watching the sunrise or sunset. We even carved out a shortcut over King's Chair Hill to town and school. This home was more than just a place to live—it was a labor of love and a reflection of my parents' vision for a life rooted in nature, simplicity, and family.

Chadron felt like the middle of nowhere—or, as my mom liked to say, "where Jesus left his shoes." With a modest population of just 6,000 people, Chadron State College stood as an educational oasis for the surrounding area. It was a lifeline for many, though plenty of our classmates left for bigger universities with more opportunities. That same yearning for something more is what led me to take the chance to go to New York.

My sisters were my whole world. I have three of them—Susan, Georgia, and Elizabeth—and while we share a deep bond, we're all very different. Susan, the oldest, is incredibly smart and a talented drummer. She was studying criminal justice with a minor in music, combining her intellect and creativity. Georgia, next in line, was forging her own path at the University of Nebraska-Lincoln on the opposite side of the state. She's a free spirit who has always known exactly what she wants. When she sets her mind to something, there's nothing she can't accomplish. I'm the third sister, and then there's Liz, the youngest. She was coming home to finish her senior year of high school after spending a year as an exchange student in Finland. Liz and I had shared a room our entire lives until she left for Finland, and I missed her terribly. I couldn't wait to have her back home again.

Flying back home was a long journey. We flew into Denver, Colorado, where my aunt and uncle picked us up and drove the five hours to Chadron. The very next morning, I had to register for classes. Susan gave me a ride into town on the back of her motorcycle. Although we lived just behind the college, the roads didn't cut over the hill, making it a surprisingly long drive. Growing up, those hills were how I fell in love with running. I'd often take the trails over King's Chair Hill as a shortcut to school, avoiding the longer gravel road that wound through Hidden Valley and onto Maple Street. It was faster, and the quiet beauty of the trails became my escape.

I also had a motorcycle of my own, but more often than not, I'd ride with Susan. We'd bounce along the washboard gravel road into town, singing, chatting, or simply soaking in the fresh air tinged with the sweet scent of alfalfa.

That day, everything felt different. The sky looked bluer, the air smelled fresher, and the countryside stretched out as if it had grown larger in my absence. It was good to be home. After registering for classes, Susan and I stopped by M Hall, the music building, to catch up with some of her friends in the music department. Susan was a talented drummer, playing in concert, jazz, pop, and just about every other kind of band. I had signed up for band as an elective that year, but I wasn't anywhere near her level.

We stood in the entryway chatting with her friends. At a school as small as ours, everyone seemed to know each other. Susan and I drew a bit of attention with our stories about our summer adventures in New York City. Then someone asked if we'd heard about John Webb, the jazz band instructor who was on sabbatical. We all knew John, his wife Toni, and their daughter Monique. They lived just a block from M Hall, and we'd been to their house many times. Toni and my mom were friends. John had been Susan's jazz band instructor for years, so I was surprised to hear he'd be away. However, it made sense. He was pursuing his PhD at the University of Northern Colorado (UNC), known for its exceptional music program. Under Gene Aitken's direction, their jazz band had been nominated for several Grammys. That's how good they were.

"Do you want to meet his replacement?" someone asked us.

"Sure, why not?" I said, standing there windblown from the motorcycle ride, wearing shorts and a t-shirt. I wasn't expecting much. In my mind, John's substitute was bound to be some stodgy, polyester-clad band director.

But then *he* walked in.

Brian.

He wasn't wearing polyester. He had on a linen shirt with the sleeves casually rolled up, cool baggy pants, and effortlessly stylish shoes. He was everything I wasn't expecting. Even more surprising? He had the same funky haircut as me—short and spiked. And he was gorgeous.

The moment our eyes met, I swear the Earth shifted. We exchanged hellos, and in that instant, something electric passed between us. The attraction was immediate, undeniable, and utterly consuming. That moment changed everything. There are events in life so defining, so significant, that you can divide time into "before" and "after." Meeting Brian was one of those moments for me. I didn't know it was coming, but on that warm August day in 1988, standing in the entryway of M Hall, I met the love of my life. And nothing has ever been the same since, marking everything in my life that came before that moment and after.

Suddenly, the school year was looking a lot brighter. I couldn't wait to see Brian again. After moving into the dorms, I settled into a full schedule of classes, but what I looked forward to most was band. Meeting several times a week, it gave me the perfect excuse to be in M Hall, even though I wasn't in the jazz band or any of Brian's classes. Still, I clung to the hope of bumping into him. I made a point of arriving at the band early, and he seemed to make a point of being in the hall when I did. He was absolutely captivating; gorgeous and magnetic, with a charisma that drew me in completely. Every time he looked at me, I felt butterflies fluttering in my stomach, the same butterflies I still feel now when I think about those moments.

It was clear he was just as happy to see me as I was to see him.

The first weekend back, I went home to spend time with my mom and unwind. Sitting outside in the sun, I let myself recharge, soaking up the warmth and the peace of being home. I'd listen to the *American*

Top 40 countdown with Casey Kasem, one of my favorite rituals. The best part was always the Long-Distance Dedication—each week, someone would write in with a heartfelt love story and dedicate the perfect song to express their emotions. The lyrics to those love songs, the ones about unbreakable devotion, where no mountain was too high or river too deep to keep lovers apart, always resonated with me. Even as a kid, I knew love was the most important thing in my life. I knew that someday, I'd experience a love like that.

I'd had boyfriends before, but they were just that—boyfriends. I cared about them, but I knew deep down it wasn't love. I wasn't even looking for love then. I was trying to figure out my life, to become someone I could be proud of—someone worthy of a great love. I had promised myself to focus on my studies during my freshman year, but that promise was already being tested. Thoughts of Brian, the man I had just met, were sneaking into my mind more often than I'd like to admit. To clear my head and refocus, I went home to see my mom.

That's when I heard voices—someone was walking up the driveway. We lived out in the country, and our home wasn't the kind of place people dropped by on a whim. Our driveway was a steep, winding climb across five acres, and getting to the top wasn't for the faint of heart. Just before the steepest stretch, there was a "pull-off" area—designed as a safe spot to stop if your car couldn't make the climb. You either dropped the car into first gear and gunned it to the top, or you pulled off and walked the rest of the way. Over the years, we'd seen plenty of friends hesitate at the last moment, only to spin their tires, dig into the gravel, and create craters they couldn't escape. Some even had to back down the hill in defeat. Once, someone lost control entirely and crashed right through the pull-off fence.

So, when I heard voices coming up the driveway, my heart skipped a beat. Could it be Brian?

Sure enough, as I glanced out, there they were—Toni Webb and Brian, walking up the hill toward the house.

Brian was filling in for John, teaching all of his classes for the year while living in John and Toni's house. With Toni and John preparing to leave for Colorado the following week, Toni took it upon herself to play matchmaker before heading out. She went inside to "visit with my mom," leaving me to show Brian around. I led him through my sanctuary nestled on the side of the hill—a place I called home. We walked along the paths I had helped create, eventually making our way to the bench at the point. It was my favorite spot, situated at the end of the walkway, offering a stunning panoramic view of the countryside. The sunsets there were magical.

Brian and I sat down on the bench, and as we talked, we found ourselves falling for each other. Our conversation flowed effortlessly, as though we'd known each other forever. We talked about everything—our shared dreams of traveling, our passion for experiencing life to the fullest. The sun beat down on us, making it hot on that August afternoon, but I wouldn't have moved for anything.

Brian told me about his life. At 27, he was the eldest of four siblings and came from a small town in North Dakota, where his family still lived. For the past four years, he had been in Greeley, Colorado, earning his master's degree at UNC. A talented saxophonist, he was preparing to audition for the Conservatory of Music in Bordeaux, France, to study with the world-renowned classical saxophone instructor Jean-Marie Londeix. This sabbatical teaching position was a perfect fit for him while he waited for his audition.

As he shared his dreams, hopes, and plans, I listened, captivated—not just by his words but by the depth of his passion. He wasn't just passionate about music; he loved life, history, tennis, and art. Though

I was young, I understood the weight of what was happening between us. This wasn't just a moment; it was a turning point.

The connection between us was undeniable and immediate, more profound than just physical attraction. As we sat on that bench, we shared thoughts and feelings that only two people destined to love each other could. In his eyes, I saw my soulmate, and I knew he saw the same in mine.

I didn't want the afternoon to end. That spot became something even more special that day. The bench at the point would forever be the "love bench" to me, the place where my life shifted, and love truly began.

My thoughts were consumed by Brian, leaving little room for anything else. So much for my plan to focus on my studies, but I was completely head over heels for him. I couldn't stop smiling, couldn't sleep, couldn't eat, and found it nearly impossible to concentrate on school. All I wanted was to spend every moment with him. Still, I worried about the implications of our relationship in such a small town. He was an instructor, and I was just a freshman. It felt complicated, even risky. One day, I asked my mom what she thought about the idea of Brian and me dating. Without missing a beat, she said, "I don't mind at all, as long as you date in Denver."

But the connection between us was undeniable, and resisting it felt futile. Every afternoon, we found a way to meet in the hallway at M Hall. Sometimes, I'd show him pictures from my summer in New York; other times, we'd spend the time flirting, laughing, and getting lost in each other's company. It didn't matter what we were doing—neither of us could get enough.

Brian asked me out to dinner and a movie. Was he serious? Of course, I wanted to go! Dinner, a movie, and maybe dancing afterward? He could have asked me to marry him right then, and I'm pretty sure my answer would have been an enthusiastic "YES!"

The next 24 hours felt like an eternity as I waited for our date. I tried to stay busy with classes and my job at the Child Development Center, but my thoughts were completely consumed by Brian. Finally, the moment arrived. He came to my dorm room to pick me up, and he looked incredible. Standing tall at 5'9" (with my spiked hair giving me a little extra height), I was thrilled to see that he was an easy 6 feet tall—and his spiked hair rivaled mine. We had a similar style, and as we stood there together, it was clear: we just *looked right* together.

I was a bundle of nerves and excitement, overwhelmed by feelings I'd never experienced before. As we drove to dinner, Brian put on The Police and started singing along. He had a great voice and this magnetic, playful energy. He drummed on the steering wheel and dashboard, even tapping the ceiling for a crash cymbal. I was so giddy inside I could barely speak.

When we arrived at the restaurant, we immediately ran into several of his Jazz Band students, and all eyes were on us. Then, as if that wasn't enough, we got to the movie theater, and who should sit directly behind us but the Dean of the Music Department and his wife. Of all the seats in the entire theater, they picked the ones right behind ours. We made polite small talk, but it was hard to relax. After the movie, neither of us wanted the night to end, so we went for a walk. By then, my silence had started to confuse him. He thought there was this undeniable connection between us; it was something magical, and then suddenly, I was so quiet. "Aren't you having a good time?" he asked.

I admitted I was nervous. I was having the time of my life, and I didn't want to ruin it by saying something awkward or embarrassing. That's when he took me in his arms and kissed me. And oh, what a kiss it was. In that moment, everything changed. I've never been the same since.

After that night, September 2, 1988, we were inseparable. Love found us, and we surrendered to it wholeheartedly. We didn't question the connection; it was undeniable. How do you explain love at first sight? You can't—it simply happens. Looking into Brian's eyes, I saw my soul mate, and he saw his. It felt as though the universe had conspired to bring us together, and we willingly embraced its pull.

That fall was a beautiful whirlwind. Though both of us were busy with classes, we spent every moment we could together. We exchanged love letters, cards, and flowers, each day feeling more magical than the last. Every morning, I woke up with a renewed sense of joy, eager to see him and make new memories.

I lived in the dorms, and Brian stayed at John's house, sharing the space with John's daughter and a few students renting the basement. Privacy was scarce, but we didn't let that stop us. We met in his office, went for long walks and drives, and made the most of every chance to be together.

I often worried about how our relationship might be perceived in such a small town and how it could impact his job. But Brian brushed those concerns aside. "This job is temporary," he'd remind me. "You're forever." His certainty and devotion steadied me, allowing me to cherish the love we were building.

Brian's passion for music was infectious, and under his leadership, the Jazz Band flourished. Student recitals and weekly performances became highlights of the semester. He made a lasting impression on both our small college and the town. His energy as a director was magnetic; his every movement was brimming with intensity. He threw his entire body into directing, bouncing around the stage, and drawing out the best in his students. His enthusiasm inspired everyone to rise to his high expectations.

Still, nothing matched his love for playing the saxophone. While his students admired him as a teacher and conductor, few had actually heard him perform. That would change with his faculty recital—a moment that promised to reveal the depth of his talent and passion to all.

Brian's love for music was woven into his upbringing. His father played drums in a polka band, so music was in his blood. As a child, Brian was captivated by *The Lawrence Welk Show*, which introduced him to a variety of musicians and styles. He developed an appreciation for all genres—classical, jazz, pop, and Big Band among his favorites.

From an early age, his talent was undeniable, but it wasn't until high school that he began to take music seriously. His dedication paid off, earning him numerous honors as a saxophonist. Remarkably, he even played with the college band while still in high school, showcasing his exceptional ability.

After earning his bachelor's degree in North Dakota, Brian moved to Greeley, Colorado, to study at the University of Northern Colorado. There, he trained under the legendary Gene Aitken and Roger Greenberg, two of the best in the field. His time at UNC was transformative. He excelled in his studies and achieved the coveted first chair in Jazz Lab Band 1—an extraordinary honor. The band recorded albums and even received Grammy Award nominations, a testament to their incredible skill.

I learned all of this much later because Brian never bragged. He was deeply humble, preferring to let his music speak for itself. He insisted his students call him Brian, saying he wouldn't care for a title even if he had a PhD. Yet, beneath that humility lay a relentless perfectionist, someone who held himself to the highest standards.

The night of Brian's faculty recital, our second-month anniversary, was unforgettable. We had dinner together at his place beforehand, and I expected him to be nervous. But he wasn't. Instead, he told me he was excited to perform for me, finally, and dedicated his recital to me. I was deeply touched. After wishing him luck, I found my seat in the audience, butterflies fluttering in my stomach.

As the lights dimmed, Brian stepped onto the stage, flanked by music stands brimming with sheet music. His accompanist, the college's piano instructor, took their place at the piano. From the moment Brian stood under the spotlight, he exuded confidence and command. And when he began to play, I was captivated. I wasn't prepared for what I heard. His talent was nothing short of extraordinary—far beyond anything I had expected from him or anyone. The sheer beauty and power of his performance left me spellbound. As I watched him, a wave of self-doubt crept in. What did this incredible, gifted man see in me?

It hit me that Brian wasn't destined to stay in a small town. He was meant for a much larger stage, and a life filled with travel, music, and all the dreams we had talked about together. I prayed that I would be enough for him, that I could share in that life and support his aspirations. He already had my heart, and in that moment, I knew I was ready to do whatever it took to nurture and stand by him.

In addition to directing the Jazz Band, Dixieland Band, and giving lessons, Brian also led the Combos—small bands that played popular music and hosted dances for the college and surrounding communities. When Brian sang, we got to see the true performer in him. He had *it*—that special mix of charisma and talent that captivates an audience. Although he often sang casually in the car with me, seeing him on stage was something else entirely. Once he had the microphone in hand, it was nearly impossible to take it away from him. Many nights, I found myself dancing near the stage, completely mesmerized as he sang directly to me. Even in a room full of people, his gaze never wavered—his eyes found mine, and in that moment, it was as if no one else existed. When Brian looked at me, my spirit soared. I was his completely, and he was mine.

On weekends, we often took trips together, usually driving to Colorado. Brian wanted to show me the town he had called home for the past four years, the mountains, and to escape the small-town routine for a while. The car became our little world, a private bubble where it was just the two of us. Those long road trips were some of the happiest moments of my life. We filled the hours with music, singing along to our favorite songs, talking about everything and nothing, and laughing until our sides hurt. It didn't matter where we were headed or how long the drive took—what mattered was that we were together.

Brian was incredibly romantic. When he wasn't writing me heartfelt poems—he wrote many—he would find the perfect lyrics from love songs to express how he felt. He sang to me often, brought me flowers, and gifted me cassette tapes filled with songs he wanted to share. One of the most meaningful gestures was when he created compilation tapes of his favorite classical pieces. Along with each tape, he included detailed notes explaining what the composer was trying to convey or describing the emotions the music evoked in him. It made me feel truly special that he wanted to share everything with me—his music, his thoughts, his feelings, and, most importantly, his time.

In October, I was unexpectedly hospitalized due to severe anemia. I was in excruciating pain and slipping in and out of consciousness. My mom showed up at my dorm with the doctor to convince me to go to the hospital—I didn't want to go, but I had no choice. I don't even remember how I got from my dorm to the hospital, but I do remember waking up to see my mom and Brian by my bedside. Apparently, my mom had called Brian and told him I was sick. I'd tried to keep our relationship hidden from her, thinking she wouldn't approve, but she already knew. As she put it, "A mother always knows."

Brian stayed with me through it all, even when I wasn't fully conscious. Although I was only in the hospital for one night and a day, he never left my side. I'll never forget the moment he stood outside my hospital window and serenaded me, singing in front of everyone. It made me smile and feel more loved than I ever thought possible. It was a gesture so beautiful; it still fills my heart every time I think about it.

By November, we were tired of constantly running back and forth between my dorm and his house, so we decided to rent a place of our own. We found a small trailer close to campus. It wasn't anything fancy, but it gave us the privacy we craved.

One evening, Brian planned one of the most romantic surprises of my life. He blindfolded me and led me to the park just before sunset. The sky was a serene blend of orange and purple, casting a dreamy glow. He walked me quite a distance before finally removing the blindfold. There, in front of me, was a Pine tree with a heartfelt declaration of our love carved into its bark: a heart with our initials inside. Brian had painstakingly carved it himself, using his reed knife during breaks between classes. That simple, timeless gesture took my breath away. That tree became our special spot. Whenever we could steal a moment away from our busy lives, we would meet there, under the shade of its branches, and be reminded of the love we had etched into its bark, and into our lives.

As the deadline for Brian's application to the Conservatory drew near, he made the tough decision to invest in a new saxophone. The instrument he had used throughout his college career was more than just a tool; it was his voice, an extension of himself. However, his instructor, Roger Greenberg, was traveling to Paris in December, and while there, he could personally select a top-tier Selmer saxophone, crafted to perfection at the very source. The opportunity to upgrade to an instrument of that caliber was too good to pass up, despite the sentimental attachment to his old one.

When Mr. Greenberg called to let Brian know the new saxophone had arrived, we made arrangements to deliver his old one to a promising young talent in Cheyenne, Wyoming, on our way. Watching Brian say goodbye to his old horn was profoundly moving. That saxophone had been more than an instrument; it had been his voice, his companion, and his life for the past decade. It had carried him through so many milestones in his career. Seeing him so introspective and emotional only made me love him more, as it showed the depth of his connection to his craft and his willingness to honor it.

Brian took comfort in knowing the saxophone would continue its journey in the hands of a gifted young musician, but the drive began in thoughtful silence as he processed the change. Gradually, his mood shifted, and with each mile, his excitement for the new saxophone grew. This was more than an upgrade; it was the beginning of a new chapter for him. His saxophone wasn't just an instrument; it was his passion, his livelihood, and the center of his creative world. He looked forward to the new tone, the possibilities it would unlock, and all the music it would create—not just for him, but for us.

Mr. Greenberg had gone above and beyond, carefully testing countless saxophones in the Paris shop to find the one with the finest quality. He even admitted, with a touch of envy, that he wished it were his instead of Brian's. When the moment finally came for Brian to open the case, he sat quietly on the couch, the blue case resting on his lap. He took a deep, steadying breath before lifting the lid. As he held the saxophone for the first time, his eyes sparkled with pure joy. The emotion in the room was palpable. When he pulled his mouthpiece from his pocket and played her for the very first time, the sound was breathtaking. His face lit up with exhilaration, and I was moved to tears by the beauty of it all, his connection to the instrument, the fulfillment of a dream, and the sheer joy radiating from him. It was a moment that will forever be etched in my memory.

In early December, Brian finalized his application to Mr. Londeix, carefully preparing a compilation of his best performances. The tape included selections from his Master's recitals, showcasing his jazz expertise on both the alto and soprano saxophones, as well as highlights from his faculty recital, where his classical artistry shone. The recordings demonstrated the full range of his skill, passion, and versatility. That envelope held more than just an application—it carried his talent, ambition, and dreams. Together, we said a heartfelt prayer before sending it off to Bordeaux, France, with all our hopes resting on its journey.

The winter holidays arrived, and aside from a trip to visit Brian's family, there was little to distract him from the long, anxious wait for news. Since our first date, we had hardly spent a moment apart, filling our time with conversations about our dreams and plans for the future—*our* future. I had spoken with Brian's mom on the phone a few times and even exchanged letters with her, but Christmas break gave us the perfect opportunity to meet in person. Brian was eager to take me home, and I was just as excited to go.

The drive to Hope, North Dakota, was long, but as always, we enjoyed every mile together. Brian's parents lived in the house where he had grown up, a cozy and familiar place full of memories. His youngest sister was still in high school, while his oldest sister, now married with a family of her own, lived nearby. Their brother was in Fargo. Though Brian had been away for years, going home for Christmas still carried the excitement and nostalgia of childhood. It was heartwarming to see Brian in his role as a son and brother, sharing stories, laughter, and traditions with his family. He took me on a tour of his old haunts and introduced me to some of his longtime friends. Watching him in his element, surrounded by people who had known him all his life, gave me an even deeper appreciation of the man I loved.

Our time in Hope was brief, but during those few precious days, Brian knelt down on one knee and asked me to marry him. He was so sweet, so romantic, and so sincere. Though the future was uncertain, whether he'd be accepted to the Conservatory or need to find another teaching position, one thing was clear: wherever life took him, he wanted me by his side. His words filled my heart, and I knew, without hesitation, that my answer was *yes*. I wanted to be his wife.

Marriage wasn't a new topic for us—we had talked about our future often, and it was always a shared vision, *our* future. But this moment solidified everything we had been dreaming of together. Unlike many, I didn't want an engagement ring. Brian knew that about me. I wasn't interested in traditional symbols or formalities. There was no dowry, no reciprocal engagement ring for him, and to me, a ring wasn't what mattered. What I wanted was him, our commitment, and the promise of a life shared. I longed for the deeper meaning of a wedding band and the covenant of marriage, and the feeling that comes with it, the partnership that it represents. Falling in love so young hadn't been part of my plan, but love has a way of rewriting the story. Meeting Brian, *loving* Brian, was unexpected yet undeniably right. Though I wanted to shout our engagement from the rooftops, we agreed to keep it just between us for now. This moment, this promise, felt too sacred and special to share just yet.

We wanted to make time to celebrate Christmas with my family as well. After spending Christmas Eve with Brian's family, we set out on Christmas Day to head back home for the remainder of the holiday. Brian was running a fever and clearly unwell, but he was determined to ensure I could spend Christmas with my family. I suggested we wait a day or two until he felt better, but he wouldn't hear of it. Despite how miserable he must have felt, he drove us home because he wanted to see me happy. It broke my heart to see him push through his discomfort for my sake, but it also made me love him even more. He loved me so deeply, so completely, and I felt it in every word he spoke, every glance he gave me. Even in his quiet, selfless acts, his love shone through. In that moment, and every moment with him, I felt like the happiest person alive.

Having my sisters home for the holidays made everything feel even more special. I cherished the time we spent together, especially since Georgia was home from the university for just a few days. I couldn't keep Brian's proposal to myself any longer. I had to tell someone. Bursting with joy, I confided in her, making her promise not to say a word. I wanted to be the one to tell my parents, but I wasn't sure how they would react. Georgia was thrilled for me, though she didn't fully realize how serious Brian and I were. This was actually the first time she'd met him, so it all felt new to her. Susan, on the other hand, was already a good friend of Brian. They not only shared their passion for music but also played tennis together. And because we spent so much time at my house, Brian was already close with my mom and my youngest sister, Liz.

The holidays provided a welcome distraction for Brian, but he still dedicated hours each day to practicing as he anxiously awaited news from Mr. Londeix. With each passing day, the anticipation grew, and collecting the mail became a ritual we shared, ensuring we'd be together when the letter arrived. Finally, on a cold January evening, the moment we'd been waiting for arrived. A single envelope in the mailbox held our answer. We held our breath and said a quick prayer before Brian carefully opened it. He was visibly nervous, but I was unwavering in my confidence. I just knew the letter would contain the acceptance he had worked so hard for. And it did. Tears streamed down our faces as we read the words confirming Brian's acceptance as one of only 12 students worldwide selected to study with Mr. Londeix that fall. He was in! Bordeaux, France, was no longer a distant dream; it was real. We hugged, kissed, and jumped with joy, caught in the euphoria of the moment. It was his dream come true, and

I couldn't have been prouder. We called everyone we knew to share the incredible news. All of Brian's relentless hard work had paid off.

The Conservatory was tuition-free, thanks to France's commitment to supporting the arts and education. Brian would only need to cover his living expenses for the year. From the very beginning, Brian spoke of "us" and "we." He couldn't imagine going to France without me, and I couldn't fathom being apart for an entire year. We didn't know exactly how we'd make it work, but one thing was sure: we were going to France—together.

The spring semester was a whirlwind. I juggled a full course load with a part-time job, while Brian's schedule was more packed than ever. He taught for long hours and spent even more time practicing, determined to continue growing as a musician and teacher. One of the highlights of the semester was the Jazz Festival hosted by UNC, Brian's alma mater. He brought his jazz band to perform and be evaluated by some of the most esteemed instructors in the field— mentors he deeply admired. The stakes were high, and Brian felt the pressure. He poured himself into selecting the perfect repertoire for his students and led countless extra rehearsals to ensure they were fully prepared. When the big day arrived, all the hard work paid off. The band delivered a standout performance, earning glowing feedback from the judges. John, the instructor on sabbatical, was in the audience and was astonished by the transformation of his former students under Brian's leadership. For Brian, the festival was a triumph. Hearing praise from the mentors he respected so deeply was profoundly validating. It was a moment of pride and recognition that underscored just how far he'd come.

Throughout the year, I stayed in touch with my aunt and cousins in New York. My cousin had been hoping I would return in the summer to work as a nanny again. When I wrote to let her know I wouldn't be coming back, I explained that I was in a serious relationship with Brian and that we were planning to move to France in the fall. Not long after sending the letter, Brian and I were visiting my mom when she suddenly asked us to step outside to talk. Her tone was serious, and I felt a wave of nervousness wash over me. What could she possibly want to say?

It turned out my aunt had called her after receiving my letter, asking if Brian and I were planning to get married. Caught off guard, I hadn't even mentioned marriage in the letter, except that I wouldn't be returning for the summer, and my cousin needed to find another nanny. But now, standing hand in hand with Brian, my mom looked at us intently and asked if it was true. She went on to say that she would not allow me to leave the country with him unless we were married. I was taken aback. On one hand, I was irritated that my aunt had jumped to conclusions about us getting married. On the other hand, my mom's ultimatum put everything into sharp focus. I finally told her the truth: we did want to get married, but I had been afraid she would object because I was so young.

It was a relief to finally share our plans with my mom. I think deep down she already knew. We talked about marriage constantly, and it was obvious how serious we were about each other. We told her we wanted a simple outdoor wedding at "the point," where the "love bench" was, the very place we had fallen in love. We decided on our anniversary, September 2nd, as the perfect date. Just like that, it was settled. However, my mom insisted on one tradition: Brian had to formally ask my dad for permission. I rolled my eyes at the idea, but Brian didn't hesitate to agree. My dad worked for the railroad and lived two hours away, so we planned a trip the following week to have dinner with him and make it official. I had never seen Brian so nervous. We made it through dinner, but when the moment came, he couldn't bring himself to ask. We even ordered dessert to give him more time. My mom had led us to believe my dad might oppose the idea, but when Brian finally worked up the courage, my dad was gracious and gave us his blessing. He had one request only: I promise to finish my education. I could take a year off while we were in France, but once we returned, I would enroll at the university wherever Brian's career took him.

It was so simple. Everything about our plans, our future, and our love felt uncomplicated and natural. Together, we knew we could handle anything.

Chapter Two
Leaving Home, Finding Us

Summer vacation began in the second week of May. With Brian's teaching duties wrapped up and my semester complete, we decided to move to Greeley, Colorado, together for the summer despite my mother's disapproval. She strongly opposed the idea of us living together before marriage, but I decided to go anyway. I had always been a responsible and trustworthy person. I didn't drink or stay out late, and she had never needed to discipline me. I worked hard to maintain good grades, participated in sports, and held a part-time job since I was 13. I wasn't one to rebel or defy her wishes, but this time was different. Brian and I didn't share her views on "living in sin." We both knew our commitment to one another ran deeper than societal conventions. A marriage certificate wasn't going to change how much we loved, respected, or cherished each other. We had already made those promises in our hearts. While we both valued romance, we also understood that it was our actions and responsibility to one another that truly mattered. Living together wasn't something we saw as immoral; it was simply the next step in building our life together. Spending the summer apart wasn't an option, and we were ready to face whatever came our way—together.

Brian found an apartment directly across the street from the UNC music building, sub-leased from an acquaintance who was spending the summer in South America. It was the perfect location for him to focus on practicing and taking lessons with Mr. Greenberg.

Living in Greeley was an exciting new chapter for us. It was my first time truly living away from my family. While I had spent summers away before, it had always been with one of my sisters. This felt different, as it was an essential step in preparing myself for the much bigger leap of moving to France. There were moments when homesickness hit me hard. Brian, having never experienced it himself, couldn't fully understand what I was feeling. Still, he held me close, comforting me with his presence and quiet reassurances. His support made all the difference, and it helped me navigate the growing pains of living independently for the first time.

Brian's days were intense, practicing for eight hours, giving lessons, and taking lessons himself. Mr. Greenberg and I both knew he didn't really need the lessons; what he needed most was confidence in his own abilities. Sometimes, I'd sit outside his practice room and listen to him play. Even when he was running through scales, his sound was extraordinary. I had never encountered talent like his before, and every time I heard him play, I was in awe all over again.

Meanwhile, I spent my days working at a restaurant. It wasn't the greatest job, but it helped cover the bills. Coming home was always a joy, though Brian had a habit of leaving sweet notes on the door for me, little messages saying he loved me or inviting me to listen to a new tape he'd discovered. He was always so eager to share the things he loved, and it made me feel incredibly special.

Most evenings, we spent together savoring each other's company and the peaceful simplicity of our time together. On weekends, we took short trips to the mountains and explored nearby towns. Brian showed me his favorite old haunts, the majestic peaks, and the vibrant streets of Boulder. We both fell in love with that artsy little town nestled in the foothills of the Rockies. It felt alive with creativity and charm, but in truth, it didn't matter where we went or what we did. We were so deeply in love that every moment felt special just because we were together. Before we knew it, the summer had slipped by in a blissful blur.

We didn't own much, and by August, we even sold Brian's car. It didn't make sense to store it for a year while we were abroad, and the extra money was essential. We were living on a tight budget and had to borrow funds to cover our living expenses for the coming year. As summer came to a close, my sister Susan drove to Greeley to pick us up and take us home for our wedding. Everything was falling into place, one step at a time.

I never spent my days dreaming of a wedding; instead, I dreamed of finding true love. When I met Brian, he exceeded every hope and dream I'd ever had. To us, our wedding day wasn't about tradition but a private moment to declare our eternal love. We had already spent the entire year expressing that love in countless ways. A grand, traditional wedding wasn't what we wanted. Instead, we envisioned standing together under the vast blue sky, surrounded by a cathedral of pine trees, at the very spot where we first fell in love. It was simple, pure, and exactly what we wanted—a celebration of the love that had already transformed our lives.

One challenge we faced was finding someone to officiate our wedding. We didn't belong to a church, and the Justice of the Peace wouldn't leave his office. Desperate, we asked a friend's father, who was an attorney, if he could perform the ceremony, but he politely declined, saying he "didn't do weddings." As a last resort, we found a minister willing to help because Brian's Dixieland band had played for her youth group a couple of times during the year. She was new to officiating and, in fact, this would be her first wedding. When we met with her before the ceremony, it became glaringly obvious she had a crush on Brian. She flirted shamelessly with him, barely acknowledging my presence. It was awkward and absurd, but we had no other options. She asked Brian all the questions, going out of her way to mention she used to be a swimsuit model. We had to bite our lips and squeeze each other's hands to keep from laughing at how ridiculous the situation was, watching her attempt to flirt with the groom right in front of his fiancée!

I tried on several dresses at local boutiques but couldn't find one I liked, so I sketched a design and found a seamstress to bring it to life. It was one-of-a-kind, just like I wanted. Instead of choosing between my three sisters, I asked my childhood friend Pam to be my maid of honor. Pam and I had been friends since kindergarten and stayed close over the years. She even flew in to be there for me. Brian's best man was his friend Ed, someone he'd grown close to at UNC.

My mom found someone to make our wedding cake, a beautiful white chocolate creation with a raspberry filling. My dad and his friend built a wooden walkway from the front porch to the point, serving as our aisle. There were more details to figure out than I had anticipated, more than I really cared to manage. I wasn't interested in things like the font style on invitations or the design of thank-you cards. It was supposed to be a simple day, focused on us and the love we shared. However, as plans progressed, the day started to morph into a more traditional wedding than we'd envisioned. Low-key, yes, but still filled with all the customary elements we had wanted to avoid. What was meant to be an intimate gathering of family and close friends ended up including nearly everyone from the music department. It all started to feel overwhelming. The only thing I truly cared about was saying my vows to Brian. At one point, I even asked him if he wanted to elope, and I wasn't joking. I just wanted to escape all the chaos. A week before the wedding, I went to pick Brian up from his practice at M Hall. The moment I saw him, my eyes filled with tears. When he gently asked what was wrong, I completely broke down. Everything was spiraling into a bigger production than I ever wanted. I didn't care about the fuss or the details; I just wanted to run away. But Brian, with his love and patience, talked me out of it. He reminded me of all the time and effort my family had put into making the day special, the money they had spent, and how far so many of our loved ones were traveling to share this moment with us. He was right. Running away would have been a mistake—a knee-jerk reaction to the stress. I realized how much I would have regretted eloping. I might not have cared about the details, but I did care deeply about the people who were there to celebrate with us. Brian's calm reassurance grounded me, and together, we faced the final days of planning with a renewed sense of gratitude.

One of my high school friends called to congratulate me after receiving the wedding invitation. We hadn't seen each other since graduation because she went to college out of state. During our chat, she mentioned she was a little surprised to hear I was "settling down." I stopped her right there and made it clear that there was no settling involved. I explained that we weren't buying a house or starting a family anytime soon; in fact, we were just getting started. This gorgeous, talented man had swept me off my feet, and we were madly in love. We were about to embark on an incredible adventure, moving to France for a year to chase our dreams. This love affair was beyond anything I had ever imagined. I told her I was happier than I ever thought possible, and Brian was too. What we had wasn't about settling. It was about diving headfirst into a beautiful, passionate life together. "Settling down" was the furthest thing from what we were doing.

We stayed at my family's house for a couple of weeks leading up to the big day. Brian set up in the "storage room," which we converted into his temporary space, while I slept on the couch in the living room. During those weeks, Brian truly bonded with my family, especially my mom and my sister, Susan. He loved the serenity of life in the countryside, the quiet, and the natural beauty surrounding us. Inside the house, however, it was a different story: organized chaos. A foreign exchange student from Brazil, Grazi, was living with us at the time, sharing a room with Liz. The house was full of people and constant activity, but it made those last few weeks feel lively and special. It was a joyful, memorable way to spend our final days at home before the wedding.

Brian's family arrived from North Dakota the night before our wedding, marking the first time our families met. We shared a casual dinner at home, with my family of six and his family of eight gathered around the table. After dinner, a few friends dropped by, and the evening turned into an impromptu jam session. The living room became our own private club. Susan played the drums, Troy took up the guitar, April was on the keyboard, and Brian sang while my sisters and I danced. It was a lively and unforgettable night, filled with music, laughter, and the joy of two families coming together.

The night before our wedding, Brian stayed at a motel with his family and his friend Ed. Since they would be leaving the day after the wedding and we were heading abroad for the next year, it was their last opportunity to spend time together.

Our wedding was scheduled for 2 o'clock, and there wasn't much for me to prepare beforehand. With my extremely short hair and no makeup routine, all I needed to do was shower and slip into my dress. Meanwhile, Susan and her friends set up on the front porch to play music. They kicked things off with Billy Idol's *"White Wedding,"* which brought some lighthearted fun to the day. I couldn't resist joining them outside for a laugh and a little dancing. It was the perfect way to shake off any nerves.

September 2, 1989, was a warm and windy day. Our neighbor kindly shuttled guests up the steep driveway, where Brian and my sisters greeted everyone outside. By two o'clock, the guests had gathered along the wooden boardwalk that served as the aisle. Brian stood waiting at the "point," the special spot where we had fallen in love, now transformed into our altar. As my father and I stepped outside, April played *"Here Comes the Bride"* on the bells, setting a poignant and beautiful tone. Peter, our photographer, captured every moment, from my father's nervous, tear-filled eyes to my own emotions spilling over. But the second I saw Brian, everything else melted away. His eyes were filled with a love so deep and intense, I could feel it pulling me toward him. At that moment, it felt like the world had disappeared—it was just the two of us, standing together, making sacred promises. We vowed to love and cherish each other in sickness and in health, in good times and bad, for all the days of our lives.

We spent our wedding day surrounded by our friends and family, sharing heartfelt hugs, joyful tears, and well-wishes. Their happiness for us was deeply moving, and we felt fortunate to celebrate with so many loved ones. The afternoon was filled with laughter, music, dancing, and delicious food, making it a truly unforgettable experience. Looking back, I'm so grateful we didn't run off and elope. That day, filled with love and joy, is a memory I'll treasure forever.

After Brian's family, Pam, Ed, and Liz departed, we decided to do something unconventional for the day after our wedding—we went tubing down the Niobrara River with my entire family, except Liz, who had left for college. We all piled into the car and drove to Valentine, Nebraska, where we tied several oversized inner tubes together and spent the afternoon floating down the river. The weather was perfect, with the warm sun and clear skies of late summer, and we had an absolute blast. It may not have been a traditional post-wedding activity, but it was uniquely ours.

I carefully made lists and packed our bags days before leaving for France, only to unpack and repack them several times. It was incredibly challenging to fit everything we might need for an entire year, through all four seasons, into just two suitcases and one carry-on. Neither of us had ever been to France, and without the convenience of the internet back then, the world felt much bigger and more uncertain. We tried to prepare as best as we could, buying a transformer for electrical appliances like Brian's metronome, his electric razor, and our hair clippers. I managed to pack shoes, address books, clothes, and as many essentials as I could cram into the bags. Brian's saxophone counted as his carry-on, and he stuffed the case with reeds and music. By the time we were finished, the bags were so heavy we could barely lift them!

Saying goodbye to Susan was incredibly hard for both of us. We hugged tightly, cried, and promised to write letters. I've always hated goodbyes, and this one was especially tough. We had to say goodbye to so many people at once. I didn't know if I'd ever see our exchange sister, Grazi, again. While we were excited about starting our new life together, leaving everything familiar behind was bittersweet.

My mom drove us to the airport in Denver, and when we hugged goodbye, the reality of it all finally hit me. I had been so busy preparing for the wedding and our trip that I hadn't let myself fully process it. I've always been sentimental, but this farewell felt different—more final. I knew I was leaving home for good, truly spreading my wings. Though I'd visit again, I was married now, and I realized I would never live at home as I once had.

Chapter Three
Across the Threshold

T he flight from New York to Paris felt endless. Since we flew overnight, we hoped to get some rest, but our excitement made sleep nearly impossible. I dozed off a few times, but it wasn't enough to shake the anticipation. We landed in Paris at 7 a.m., stored our luggage in a locker, and hopped on the subway into the city. Despite the pouring rain, we wandered around the Bastille area, buying an umbrella and savoring our very first croissant. Determined to make the most of our first day in France, we explored as much of Paris as we could, rain and all.

The combination of jet lag, emotions, and being in a foreign country was overwhelming. By the time we boarded the last train of the night to Bordeaux, we could barely keep our eyes open. The six-hour journey felt endless. We tried to stay awake so we wouldn't miss our stop, but exhaustion won out. When we finally arrived in Bordeaux, we were too tired to do anything but find the nearest hotel and collapse. Everything felt foreign—the language, the food, the city itself. The next morning, Brian made the daunting call to our landlord to let her know we were on our way to the apartment. It was a challenging conversation, but he managed well. The French lessons he'd taken in Greeley, combined with his musical ear for pronunciation, made it sound like he understood more than he actually did. Thankfully, the landlord got the message, and we arranged to meet her at the apartment around noon.

We took a cab to the address she provided, and when we arrived, we were stunned. Our new home was less than a block from the

Garonne River, right in the heart of Bordeaux's historic district. The third-floor apartment was in a stone building that had stood since 1495—a breathtaking relic of history. I'd never seen anything like it, and the thought of living in such a remarkable place for the next year left me awestruck.

We pulled our bags from the taxi and approached the door, where a stern-looking woman was waiting for us. It didn't take long to realize she wasn't particularly fond of us. She gave us a quick but pointed once-over, clearly deciding we weren't her type of people. Oh well— we weren't there to win her over to secure a place to live for the school year. Her rapid-fire French was completely incomprehensible to me. It didn't sound like anything I had studied, and I couldn't pick out a single familiar word. With the help of a phrasebook and dictionary, we managed a halting exchange. The room we rented was a small chamber at the top of the stairs above the kitchen, which had once been the maid's quarters. Mme. LeSimple, our landlord, owned the apartment but no longer lived there. She and her husband were retired and lived in the countryside, though her family still used the apartment occasionally—or at least that's what we gathered from her explanation.

The apartment itself was like stepping into a museum—ornate, elegant, and completely out of our league. It was obvious we didn't belong. Mme. LeSimple made it equally evident that we were to stay in our designated spaces: the bedroom, the bathroom, and the kitchen. The kitchen, however, came with strict boundaries. She pointed out the tiny refrigerator, no larger than a dorm-sized one, and indicated that we were allowed a single shelf. She emphasized the importance of cleaning up after ourselves and seemed to deliver a long list of rules, most of which we couldn't fully understand. What should have been a welcome felt more like a reprimand. Her tone was cold, her demeanor strict, and her instructions endless. We felt scolded before we had even unpacked. It wasn't exactly the warm arrival we had hoped for.

Our room above the kitchen was small and modestly furnished. It had a beautiful sleigh bed, a desk, a single chair, an old armoire for our clothes, and a lamp. The best part was the window, which offered a view of the tiled rooftops stretching out toward the river.

After Mme. LeSimple left, and we collapsed onto the bed, completely drained. While the sleigh bed was charming, it quickly became apparent that it was too small for us. Brian, at just over six feet, and me, at five feet nine, were taller than most French people. The bed forced us to lie on our sides and spoon every night. That first night, though, we didn't care. We were too exhausted to notice. But for the rest of the school year, stretching out was never an option—we slept curled up every night.

That first sleep was deep and long. When we finally woke up, we were completely disoriented. We had no idea what time it was or even what day. We found ourselves in a strange apartment, in an unfamiliar city, in a country where we barely understood the language. The one thing we knew for sure? We were starving. It was dark when we ventured out to look for food. We carefully noted landmarks along the way to ensure we could find our way back. Without a map or any idea of where to go, we wandered the streets until we spotted something open. Hunger was our only guide that night. Our first meal in our new home was nothing short of bizarre. It was a simple bun and a Coke. Even managing to buy that was an adventure, relying heavily on hand signals and a leap of faith. We hadn't yet figured out the currency, let alone how it translated into dollars and cents. The unfamiliar bills, which looked more like Monopoly money than anything real, left us fumbling. In the end, we held out a few bills and trusted the vendor to give us the correct change. Satisfied enough to quiet our hunger, we walked back to the apartment, climbed the beautiful stone staircase to the third floor, and went straight to bed. Tomorrow's mission was clear: get a map of Bordeaux.

We rose with the sun, still groggy but eager to tackle the day ahead. Even the simplest tasks felt like an adventure, starting with the shower. Like many French homes, the toilet was in a separate room entirely. It was on the other side of the apartment, and to get there, we had to go down a flight of stairs, through the kitchen, across the dining room, and down a long hallway. The bathroom itself was more modern, equipped with a sink and a shower, though the shower was unlike anything we'd ever seen. It had three walls but no curtain or door on the open side. We weren't quite sure how to use it without flooding the floor, so we improvised and hoped for the best.

Feeling freshly showered and somewhat rested, we set out to explore. Bordeaux, with its population of over 600,000, was a bustling city. We lived in the historic downtown area, close to Rue Sainte-Catherine, a famous pedestrian shopping street stretching over half a mile, lined with shops and restaurants. To get our bearings, we used two landmarks: the Garonne River to the east and the towering Pey-Berland Tower at Saint-André Cathedral to the west.

While we had an entire year to wander Bordeaux's maze of charming, winding streets, our first day had a mission: find a grocery store, a bank, and other basic necessities. Our adventure had officially begun.

We managed to track down a map and locate a grocery store, which turned out to be an adventure in itself. We spent the entire day exploring our neighborhood, soaking in the sights and sounds of our new surroundings. Brian took the lead whenever we needed to ask for directions or information. He was fearless, diving into conversations with remarkable confidence. I tried to join in, but my French pronunciation was far from perfect, and I couldn't help feeling self-conscious every time I spoke. Despite my efforts, it was clear that

Brian was our unofficial spokesperson, and I was more than happy to let him take the reins.

The next day, we made our way to the Conservatory of Music. It was a long walk along the Quai, a straight route following the river through the Algerian neighborhood. While the area wasn't the cleanest or the safest, it was vibrant and full of character. The Conservatory itself was a strikingly modern building, nestled near the historic St. Michel's Cathedral, which dates back to the 14th century. Brian was nervous as we approached, knowing he was about to meet Mr. Londeix, the man whose music had inspired him for years. Dressed sharply in a freshly pressed white button-up shirt and slacks, he looked great, but his anxiety was palpable. He wanted to make a strong first impression.

When Mr. Londeix greeted us, we offered a firm handshake and did our best to muster a polite French greeting. Though he spoke some English, it was clear he felt as uncomfortable speaking it as we did speaking French. Despite the language barrier, he invited us to sit in on a lesson he was giving to one of his French saxophonists. Mr. Londeix was an intense presence. He was serious, loud, and incredibly passionate. Even without understanding every word, it was obvious he was dissatisfied with the student's performance. Brian sat next to me, visibly sweating bullets, and I could feel my own heart racing from the tension. "Let's just say..." Mr. Londeix did not leave the best first impression on me. Brian decided not to play during that first meeting. The pressure was overwhelming, and he wanted to spend some time practicing and settling his nerves before performing for such a formidable figure. After the lesson, Mr. Londeix gave us a brief tour of the Conservatory, showing us the practice rooms and classrooms. Brian's schedule for the year was packed with individual lessons, ensemble practices, and quartet rehearsals. He would be spending nearly ten hours a day in that building.

While Brian's path for the year was laid out with structure and purpose, mine was far less defined. As we walked home after that initial meeting with Mr. Londeix, it hit me: I had an entire school year ahead of me in a foreign country with nothing planned to fill my days. We had been so focused on Brian and preparing for his studies that I hadn't given much thought to how I would spend my time. The realization was both daunting and overwhelming, staring down months of unstructured time without a clear purpose or plan. Since I didn't have a student or work visa, those options were off the table. I knew I'd spend many days simply adjusting to our new life and home. I would be the one taking care of daily essentials—buying groceries, exchanging money, and managing the practicalities of living abroad. Even grocery shopping was going to be a learning curve. The kitchen setup, with its tiny refrigerator and limited storage, forced me to rethink how we approached meals. There wasn't space to stock up, so I quickly learned to buy only fresh ingredients and just what we needed for a day or two. Living on the third floor without an elevator, navigating everything on foot, and carrying groceries up those stairs was an adjustment, too. It was an entirely new way of living, simpler, more deliberate, and unlike anything I had experienced before. While I knew I'd figure it out in time, in that moment, the uncertainty ahead felt enormous.

During those first few weeks, I walked with Brian to the Conservatory every morning. Occasionally, I'd meet him for lunch, bringing something from home since he wasn't a fan of the cafeteria food. In truth, it was less about the food and more about finding any excuse to see him and spend time together. We were inseparable; each other's whole world.

Brian was one of twelve students in Mr. Londeix's ensemble, a truly international and diverse group. Among them was another American, Gary, with whom Brian quickly became close friends. The ensemble included Sylvain, Marie-Bernadette, Edwige, Nathalie, and

Christoph from France, Monique from Canada, Takashi from Japan, Nikola from Germany, Vladimir from Russia, and Patrick from Switzerland. Together, they formed a vibrant and dynamic group of musicians, each bringing their unique backgrounds and talents to the mix.

In the evenings, Brian and I would take walks together, exploring the streets of Bordeaux. One night, we heard a group of loud Americans nearby. Though their volume was a bit jarring, we were starved for conversation and connection, so we approached them. Meeting fellow Americans abroad always felt like reuniting with long-lost family, regardless of where we were from. It turned out to be a fortuitous encounter. They told us about the Bordeaux/Los Angeles Club. At this weekly gathering, the French and Americans came together to socialize, listen to speakers, enjoy performances, and discuss various topics. They encouraged us to check it out the following Tuesday, and we did.

That chance meeting turned out to be a pivotal moment. The Bordeaux/Los Angeles Club opened doors to an incredible network of friends and connections that deeply enriched our lives. Some of the people we met that very first night are still in my life more than 30 years later. The club's director, Isabelle, even offered me a chance to volunteer one afternoon a week at their library in exchange for membership fees. I gladly accepted. Not only because we couldn't afford the fees, but also because having something meaningful to do, even just one afternoon a week, felt like a lifeline. The club became my saving grace during that year, offering community, purpose, and enduring friendships.

The following Monday, I walked to the library for my first volunteer shift, practicing my introduction in French over and over in my head. Speaking French always made me nervous, especially after Mme. LeSimple mocked my pronunciation, leaving me feeling embarrassed and self-conscious. Determined to make a good impression, I stepped inside the library and was greeted by a petite woman in a gray wool suit, her black hair neatly pinned at the nape of her neck. I opened my mouth to deliver the carefully rehearsed words, but they came out as a jumbled mess. To my relief, Mme. Cazemajou, the librarian, responded in perfect English. From that moment on, I resolved never to attempt speaking French in her presence again. She was warm and gracious, and I liked her instantly.

Over the weekly meetings, I had the privilege of getting to know her better. Mme. Cazemajou had been volunteering as the librarian for several years. Her husband was the Professor of American Literature at the University of Bordeaux, and together they had traveled extensively. She was brilliant and worldly, having lived in the United States for many years while her husband taught at prestigious universities. When she spoke about her daughter, Agnes, who had married an American and lived in the States, her face softened with pride. But it was when she mentioned her five-year-old granddaughter, Zoé, that her eyes truly sparkled with joy.

Monday afternoons at the library became the highlight of my week. Not only did I enjoy every moment spent with Mme. Cazemajou, but I also relished the opportunity to borrow books. Reading became my refuge. Between the pages, I discovered adventure, knowledge, and companionship. That year, I devoured book after book, losing myself in their stories. On sunny days, I sat on old metal benches in the public park, surrounded by manicured gardens, reading for hours. Nearby, elderly men in berets lingered, reminiscent of characters from Hemingway's novels. On rainy, dreary days, I curled up indoors with a book in hand. In the evenings, when Brian's eyes were too strained from hours of studying music, I read aloud to him. Books provided me with immense comfort and a sense of purpose in a year filled with so much unfamiliarity.

Mme. Cazemajou became my literary guide. Each Monday, we talked about the books I'd read, and she always had a thoughtful recommendation for what I should explore next. After locking up the library, we'd stop at the café near her bus stop. She would treat me to a café au lait, and we'd sip our drinks, chatting warmly until her bus arrived. Those afternoons, filled with literature, conversation, and companionship, were a gift I cherished deeply.

Brian was relieved that I had found something meaningful to do with my time. He often worried about me being alone all day and enjoyed hearing the latest stories from my afternoons with Mme. Cazemajou. Our life in Bordeaux was incredibly simple. We didn't have a television, but there was a small radio in the kitchen that we listened to most evenings after dinner. For the most part, we spent our time talking about our days, taking walks, and enjoying each other's company.

Although Brian tried to do most of his practicing at the Conservatory, he occasionally practiced in our room. With no immediate neighbors in the building, his playing didn't bother anyone—except, perhaps, himself. I loved hearing him practice, but sometimes he pushed himself too hard, playing until he was completely exhausted and frustrated. It became an ongoing struggle to convince him to take breaks and step away from the saxophone. I worried about him burning out, but getting him to ease up was no small task.

At the Bordeaux/LA Club, I met many people, but one friendship that stood out was with Estelle, a young medical student. She had spent a year as an exchange student in high school in South Dakota and attended the club to keep up her English. Estelle was studying to become a doctor and, though a few years older than me, still lived with her parents and brother, as was customary in France. I was thrilled to have a new friend to spend time with and explore the city. One weekend, we even took a train trip to San Sebastián, Spain. While Brian was busy with school, I enjoyed the chance to get away and have something new and exciting to share with him when I returned.

At the club, I met several Americans living in Bordeaux, including a couple named Jill and Peter. Peter was working with the French space program, while Jill found herself in a similar situation to mine. Her husband was busy with work, leaving her on her own during the day. Jill and I quickly bonded, and our friendship has endured for more than 34 years.

Another American friend I made was Juana, who was from New Orleans. She had come to Bordeaux to immerse herself in the language, and I admired her adventurous spirit, moving to a foreign country alone, without friends or family, and embracing the experience. We spoke English together, of course, and she was a lot of fun to be around. With her help, I found a babysitting and tutoring job. Juana's brother worked with the legendary jazz trumpet player Wynton Marsalis, and when the band came through Bordeaux, she got us tickets to the performance. We even had dinner with Wynton and his band that evening. I'll never forget meeting a Grammy Award-winning musician. I told Brian that one day, people would travel far and pay good money to hear him play, too.

Through the club, I met an American woman named Linda who was looking for a nanny for her two-year-old daughter, Camille. Linda and her French husband, Olivier, lived within walking distance of our apartment, and meeting them turned out to be a true blessing. Not only did I find a job, but I also gained a wonderful friend. Taking care of Camille several days a week gave me a sense of purpose. I've always loved working with children, and since I hoped to become a mother one day, spending time with her was incredibly fulfilling.

The fall seemed to fly by. Brian was deeply immersed in his studies, and I found plenty of ways to fill my days. I got to know Bordeaux intimately, exploring its streets on foot and venturing all over the city by bus. Before long, I felt confident navigating my way around and truly began to feel at home.

For All Saints' Day, an important holiday in France, Brian and I took a trip to Paris with several of his fellow saxophone students, Patrick, Monique, and Vladimir. We all traveled together by train, gazing out the windows at the beautiful countryside rushing past. The views were unlike anything I'd ever seen, and we soaked in every moment, savoring the sights, sounds, and even the smells of the journey. Conversation was a mix of languages; Brian and I did our best with French, Monique and Patrick spoke French and a little English, and poor Vladimir struggled, as he said neither. By the time we reached the train station in Paris, Vladimir decided to part ways with us to seek out the Russian consulate.

The four of us spent three unforgettable days and two nights exploring Paris. We crammed as much as we could into our visit, marveling at landmarks like the Opera House, the Eiffel Tower, Montmartre's Sacré-Cœur, Notre Dame, the Arc de Triomphe, and the Luxembourg Gardens. We wandered through the French Quarter, sampled a variety of new foods, and created memories that would stay with us forever. Standing with Brian at the top of the Eiffel Tower felt utterly surreal. It was one of those moments that made us pause and reflect that we were living our dream, together, in one of the most iconic cities in the world.

Later in the fall, Brian, Gary, and I took a day trip to Lourdes, France, to visit the sacred grotto where Bernadette is said to have seen the Virgin Mary. Since it was the off-season, we didn't have to navigate the crowds of millions who typically visit each year. We practically had the site to ourselves. The atmosphere was peaceful and profoundly moving. The grotto itself was both humbling and awe-inspiring. We decided to walk through separately, allowing each of us to have a private moment and a personal connection to the experience. It was a visit that left a lasting impression on all of us.

As the holidays drew near, the saxophone ensemble's schedule picked up, with performances almost every week. They were preparing diligently for their big spring tour in Germany. I was lucky to attend most of their concerts and witness the incredible talent of the group. While their skill was undeniable, I have to admit that the contemporary music they often played wasn't always to my taste.

The weather in Bordeaux was mild compared to the harsh winters we were used to in the Midwest, but the constant gray skies and relentless rain throughout the winter and spring took their toll. It was dreary and oppressive—the pollution-darkened buildings and sidewalks littered with dog waste added to the grim atmosphere. I often felt unclean and out of sorts during those months. Having never lived in the heart of a city before, I missed being surrounded by nature. While there were a few parks within walking distance, the vast expanse of concrete and stone made green spaces feel like a rarity. The lack of sunlight and long winter nights only deepened our homesickness, leaving our spirits heavy.

For Christmas, Brian and I took a much-needed trip to visit our friend Coco in Germany. We had met her the year before when she was an exchange student at my hometown college. The break couldn't have come at a better time. Brian had been practicing tirelessly and performing frequently, and the strain was starting to wear on him. Meanwhile, I was grappling with homesickness. It was my first Thanksgiving and Christmas away from my family, and while letters and phone calls helped, they couldn't replace being together. Even Brian, who rarely felt homesick, admitted he missed my family. It was a challenging time for both of us, and we were ready for a change of scenery.

Although we dreamed of traveling all over Europe, our limited budget and time made that impossible. However, with Estelle's help, we found an affordable solution by arranging to share a ride with a woman driving from Toulouse to Strasbourg. We split the cost of gas, and she handled the driving, which worked out perfectly. Strasbourg was so stunning that we decided to stay an extra day to explore. We even attended Christmas Mass in the breathtaking historic cathedral. Afterward, we continued our journey by train, traveling from Strasbourg to Coco's home in Waldshut-Tiengen, Germany.

Our trip to Germany was incredible. We were captivated by the countryside and the charming towns we passed just south of the Black Forest. It was heartwarming to reconnect with my dear friend Coco and to meet her family. Their home was perched on the side of a hill, overlooking a picturesque town straight out of a Christmas card. It was absolutely stunning. Her family and friends welcomed us warmly, sharing their hospitality, traditions, and cuisine. We delighted in tasting new foods and beers, spending our days talking, dancing, and even ice skating together. Both Brian and I had a wonderful time. The break was exactly what Brian needed to recharge from his demanding schedule. By the end of the trip, we both agreed that one day, we wanted to live near the mountains.

After the Christmas holiday, the following months were intense for Brian as he focused on his studies and performances. Meanwhile, I kept busy with a couple of babysitting jobs, a tutoring session, and my ongoing involvement at the Bordeaux/Los Angeles Club. By this time, I had become so well-adjusted to life in Bordeaux that it truly felt like home. I knew exactly where to buy milk, where to find our favorite pastries, and which bus to take to get anywhere in the city. We relied entirely on walking or public transport, and we had picked up enough French to navigate daily life with confidence. As the end of our year abroad approached, we began making serious plans for what would come next.

Chapter Four
In Sickness and in Love

In the spring, the saxophone ensemble embarked on a tour, and I was fortunate to be invited along. We were deeply grateful that Mr. Londeix never hesitated to include me on the trip. As the only spouse among the twelve students, I was always welcomed and included in their plans. We traveled by bus across France and Germany, visiting cities like Freiburg, Nuremberg, Frankfurt, and others, as part of a celebration marking 100 years of the saxophone. The concerts were incredible, featuring talented musicians and composers from around the globe. While the ensemble rehearsed, I took the opportunity to explore the cities on foot, soaking in the local culture and sights. We dined at wonderful restaurants, all expenses covered, and I thoroughly enjoyed every dish I tried. Germany was an overwhelmingly positive experience for us, and the trip provided the perfect opportunity to recharge. It left us feeling refreshed and ready for the months ahead.

With close friendships, my babysitting and tutoring jobs, Brian's performances, and the saxophone tour, our days stayed full. As the spring rains faded and the sunlit hours grew longer, time seemed to fly by. Brian began applying for teaching positions at colleges and universities in the U.S., and we spent many evenings discussing where we wanted to live and how we envisioned our life together. We knew that as long as we had each other, we could make it work. I planned to take classes wherever he found a position, and together we dreamed of a life rich with experiences, art, travel, and, of course, music. We embraced the unknown and stayed open to whatever opportunities lay ahead. But the future weighed heavily on Brian. He worried constantly about finances and was determined not to rely on family for support or become a burden to anyone. Despite my reassurances that we would find a way, the pressure took its toll on him. His experiences with Mr. Londeix didn't help either. The professor's relentless criticism and harsh outbursts targeted all his students, Brian included. It was a toxic environment that left Brian physically and emotionally drained. He made a promise to himself that if he became a teacher, he would be the opposite of Mr. Londeix. His goal would be to inspire joy and passion for music rather than to tear people down with insults or perfectionist demands.

By April, the ensemble students were so burned out that they avoided practicing and each other. For the first time in Brian's life, he admitted to hating playing his saxophone. I reminded him that the end of the school year was in sight and encouraged him to persevere. I insisted he take one day off each week to do something entirely unrelated to music, though even with these small breaks, he remained utterly exhausted. I could see it in the weight he'd lost, the fatigue in his eyes, and his fading enthusiasm. While he slept often to recover, I also urged him to spend some of our remaining time in Bordeaux savoring moments together, outside of the demands and stress. One Sunday, as Brian lay in bed, too drained to move, I flung open the window to let the fresh air in and coaxed him to get up so we could explore the city together. He groaned, saying he was too tired even to get dressed. Undeterred, I said, "Fine, then I'll get you dressed myself!" With a teasing grin, I grabbed his socks and slid them onto his feet, then reached for his jeans and carefully started pulling them up his legs. It wasn't easy, and we both laughed at the effort. He looked at me with a soft expression and asked, "Would you do this for me if I couldn't dress myself?" I paused, then climbed into bed beside him, wrapped my arms around him, and rested my head on his chest. "Of course, I would," I whispered. "I'd do absolutely anything for you."

The French are well-known for their activism and protests, and their influence even extended to our stove. It had two gas burners and two electric ones, designed to keep functioning no matter which union might be on strike. While this adaptability was clever, not everything worked so smoothly. When the post office went on strike while Brian was in the middle of applying for jobs, it created a significant problem for us. It was too much to coordinate from abroad, asking my family to send out résumés and handle communication with the colleges responding to Brian's applications. After much discussion, we decided I would return to the States a month earlier than planned. That way, I could apply for teaching positions on Brian's behalf, attend Susan's college graduation, and spend time with my family. The decision made sense on paper, but I hated it. We hadn't spent any time apart in so long, and the thought of leaving Brian felt unbearable. The moment I set the date for my return ticket, regret crept in. Every fiber of my being resisted the idea of leaving him. It's a decision I can't change, but one I will always wish I could.

In late spring, Monique, Patrick, Brian, and I took a farewell trip to the beach. It was an unforgettable experience—a visit to an enormous sand dune unlike anything we'd ever seen before. For Brian, it was especially memorable as it was his first time seeing the Atlantic Ocean. We had so much fun that a couple of weeks later, Brian and I went back with Gary. There's something magical about a mountain of sand that brings out your inner child. We hiked to the top to take in the stunning view of the ocean, then let loose—rolling, cartwheeled, and running down the dune to the water below. It was pure, innocent fun, and I loved seeing Brian so carefree. In those moments, we were happy and deeply in love, savoring every bit of joy together.

In spring, the days grew long and beautiful, with sunlight lingering well past 10 p.m. in May. I was determined not to waste a single moment of the time we had left in Bordeaux. Brian and I finally embraced our inner tourists, taking pictures of the city we had come to love. We strolled through the charming streets, marveling at the architecture, reading historical markers, and making mental snapshots to carry with us for the rest of our lives. Saying goodbye to the friends I had made was especially difficult, particularly to Mme. Cazemajou. She was more than a friend—my mentor. I admired her intellect, her loving relationship with her husband, and her warm, generous spirit. We promised to write and visit one another someday. Brian and I dreamed of traveling the world, so we were certain we'd return to Bordeaux again.

As the season progressed, Brian's health worried me. He had lost even more weight, and one afternoon, his face was flushed, and his heart was racing. I made him lie down, deeply concerned. Even he admitted something wasn't right and promised to see a doctor as soon as we got back home. I knew he needed me—to remind him to eat, rest, and take care of himself when his drive to push through exhaustion got the better of him. Before I left Bordeaux, I wrote Brian a letter for every day we would spend apart. I reminded him to eat, to get some sleep, to step away from the saxophone and the conservatory now and then, and most of all, that even though we would be half a world away, I'd be thinking of him, missing him, and loving him with all my heart.

I could see how exhausted Brian was. He was worn out from playing contemporary music, what we jokingly called "honk and squeak," and tired of the monotony of our daily life. The same eleven people, the endless gray skies and rain, the dog poop littering the sidewalks, the cramped bed, and the same few outfits we'd been wearing for eight months. It was all starting to wear on him. On both of us. We were ready to go home. But once I made the decision to return early and bought my ticket, spring arrived, almost as if mocking me. The rain stopped, the skies turned a brilliant shade of blue, and suddenly, I began to feel sentimental about leaving. This place had been our home for almost a year, and now, the thought of leaving Brian behind filled me with dread. Other than the three days he spent in Angers with the saxophone ensemble, we hadn't been apart for more than a few hours.

He was my everything—my partner, my anchor, my joy. The idea of being without him felt terrifying and unbearably sad. I had a gut-wrenching feeling that I had made the wrong decision. I couldn't shake the panic. Every part of me screamed to stay, but the practicalities made it clear I should go home first. Brian and I had long, serious conversations about it, turning it over and over. Still, life doesn't come with do-overs. There's no going back, no way to undo the decisions we make, no matter how much we wish we could.

On May 10, 1990, I kissed Brian goodbye. As our lips met, I wasn't just saying goodbye to him; I was saying goodbye to the life we had built together in Bordeaux, to everything as it was.

The only thing I clearly remember about the flight home was comforting the woman sitting next to me. I reassured her there was nothing to worry about, after all, I had a bottle of holy water from Lourdes safely stowed in the overhead compartment.

My parents picked me up in Denver, and the first morning home, my mom brought me breakfast in bed. It was wonderful to see my parents and sister again, but the joy of being home felt strangely hollow without Brian. Back in the clean, crisp air, surrounded by open spaces and the vast expanse of a brilliant blue sky, I felt an ache I couldn't shake. I missed him deeply. Everything was familiar, yet everything felt wrong. I shouldn't have been there without Brian. It felt like half of me was missing.

I tried to keep myself busy. I sent out Brian's resumes, returned calls to colleges that requested interviews, and attended Susan's graduation. I wrote him letters regularly and spoke to him on the phone a few times, though the calls were brief due to the expense.

The letters I received from Brian became the only bright spot during our time apart. His beautiful love letters were filled with longing and vulnerability. He missed me as much as I missed him, but he worried that being back home and surrounded by the little comforts we had missed might distract me or make me forget about him. What he didn't realize was that none of it truly mattered without him. All the joys of being home, all the familiar pleasures, felt hollow without Brian by my side to share them. He was the source of my happiness— always had been, always would be.

Somehow, we made it through to June, marking off the days on the calendar one by one. Brian and I decided on his return flight home and planned our reunion. We focused on the moment we'd finally see each other, hold each other, and promise never to be apart again. His final exams with Mr. Londeix were intense but would be over by mid-June. I arranged to call him on Tuesday, June 12, to give him the details of his flight.

Because of the time difference, I needed to call Brian before he left for the conservatory, which meant setting my alarm for 2 a.m. I remember the alarm going off and thinking, *just 15 more minutes, then I'll get up.* But as soon as I closed my eyes again, an overwhelming feeling—almost a premonition—washed over me that something was terribly wrong. I couldn't ignore it. I had to call him. I went to the kitchen, picked up the phone, and dialed. That moment is etched in my memory. Brian answered, and the first thing he said was, "I love you, Pat." But his voice was slurred, and he didn't sound right. My heart sank.

I tried to talk to him, but something was clearly wrong. I told him to stop messing around, that he was scaring me. Desperate to make sense of it, I even asked if he had been drinking—though I knew he didn't drink. I started asking basic questions, like the dates of our birthdays, but his answers didn't make sense. My panic boiled over, and I started screaming at him to stop. By then, my voice had woken my mom and Susan. I was shaking so badly I couldn't hold the phone anymore, so my mom took over, trying to speak with Brian. As she talked to him, I crumbled, overcome with terror. Something was very wrong, and he was all alone.

Through my panic, I grabbed my address book and started calling every friend I could think of in Bordeaux. I begged Brian to stay where he was while I found help. Finally, our friend Olivier answered and went to check on him. What happened next is a blur, but somehow, Linda and Olivier managed to get Brian to their house.

Later, I learned more of what had happened in the days before that terrifying call. Gary and Estelle told me they'd had dinner with Brian the Friday before—June 6. Brian had invited them over to say goodbye and had made tacos for dinner. During the meal, he became violently ill. They took him to the hospital, where he was told it was likely the flu and was sent home. Gary stayed with him that night, but he had a weekend engagement out of town, and Estelle hadn't thought to check on him afterward.

Brian spent the entire weekend alone. By the time I spoke with him on the 12th, he had been dizzy, disoriented, and suffering from a severe headache for days. I quickly arranged for his flight home, but before he could leave, things took a turn for the worse.

The next day, Brian collapsed at Linda and Olivier's house. They called paramedics, and he was rushed to the hospital. He was admitted, and doctors began running tests to figure out what was happening to him. My heart was breaking—he was thousands of miles away, and I was powerless to help him. All I could do was wait and pray.

I canceled Brian's flight home and immediately repurchased a one-way ticket to Bordeaux. Unfortunately, I had to wait a few days before I could leave, and the waiting was agonizing. My mind raced with endless possibilities, each more terrifying than the last. Doctors speculated it could be multiple sclerosis, a stroke, Legionnaires' disease, or even mad cow disease from the hamburger in the tacos. Whatever it was, I knew it was serious, and the uncertainty only made it worse.

I flew back to Bordeaux on June 21st, and the journey felt endless and unbearable. I couldn't eat or sleep, consumed by panic and fear. At the airport, my friends Jill and Peter were there to pick me up. Jill had been visiting Brian in the hospital every day, looking after him and reminding him that I was on my way. Gary, too, was there for him daily, feeding Brian when he couldn't feed himself and offering unwavering support. Gary proved to be an incredible friend, not only caring for Brian but also packing up his belongings and cleaning our apartment. Their kindness and dedication were a lifeline during an unimaginably difficult time.

Before heading to the hospital, we stopped at Jill and Peter's apartment so I could take a moment to shower and compose myself, preparing to see the love of my life lying in a hospital bed.

The hospital in Bordeaux was a university hospital, one of the largest in Europe. As a teaching institution, it had specialists in every field of medicine, equipped with cutting-edge technology, research, and treatments. Before speaking with the doctor, I needed to see Brian. I didn't know what to expect—I just had to see him. My heart raced, my throat tightened, and I fought back the tears that seemed endless as I made my way to his room. Brian's bed was by the window, and he shared the room with another patient. At first, I didn't recognize him. He lay there with disheveled hair, and a smear of chocolate pudding lingered on his face from an earlier feeding attempt. I rushed to him and hugged him tightly. He wasn't himself—his movements and responses were slow, but he smiled, hugged me back, and whispered that he loved me. I told him I loved him, too, and promised I'd be right back. I needed to speak with the doctor, but I also had to step out of the room. I was overwhelmed, terrified, and heartbroken, yet I tried to mask my fear. I didn't want Brian to know just how scared I was.

The doctor spoke to me in English and assured me that they were testing Brian for everything. They believed he was suffering from an unknown virus that had caused an infection in his brain, encephalitis. He had a fever and was being treated with an IV antiviral medication called Zovirax (Acyclovir). The doctor explained that Brian would be moved into a private room because my presence was crucial for his recovery. While he couldn't give me a definitive diagnosis or prognosis, he was kind, patient, and appeared confident in his approach.

Remarkably, Brian responded well to my being there. He became more alert and even ate for the first time in days. Seeing him improve, even slightly, gave me a glimmer of hope. When Brian moved to a private room, I was allowed to stay with him until 9 p.m. The hospital asked me to arrive later in the morning to give the staff time to complete his care and for the doctors to make their rounds.

On my second morning back in Bordeaux, I took care of a few errands. I bought bus tickets, exchanged money for Francs, and organized some paperwork. Later, Mr. Londeix and Nathalie visited Brian, bringing fruit and music to lift his spirits. Although Brian couldn't eat because of scheduled tests, he was chewing gum and chatting. We spent time listening to music together on the Walkman. His face lit up when Prince's songs played, and when Al Jarreau's "After All" came on (our song), he hugged me tightly. I had sung those lyrics to him so many times: "After all, I will be the one to hold you, I will be the one to hold you in my arms."

I stayed with him the entire day. I fed him every meal, trying to make the food appealing since he'd lost weight. Brian was affectionate and loving, showering me with hugs and kisses whenever he was awake. When he slept, I stayed by his bedside, reading quietly. I wished I could stay through the night, but hospital rules didn't allow it. Still, I often stayed past visiting hours, and the staff kindly looked the other way. I think they understood that being together brought comfort and strength to both of us.

For the next several days, I stayed with my friends Jill and Peter. They were preparing to return to the States, so I planned to move in with Linda and Olivier afterward. Jill and Peter couldn't have been more generous. They welcomed me into their home, offering a place to shower, eat, and rest. Though I spent most of my time at the hospital, their kindness gave me a much-needed refuge. Sleep, however, didn't come easily. When I did manage to drift off, I was plagued by nightmares and began sleepwalking. More than once, I woke up in the middle of the night wandering the house, searching for Brian. That marked the beginning of many years of restless nights. True rest or relaxation seemed impossible unless Brian was by my side.

Each morning, I packed my bag with essentials for the day: the Walkman and a collection of mixtapes Susan had lovingly created for Brian, filled with his favorite music and familiar voices. We hoped it might aid his recovery. I also carried a jar of peanut butter to make sandwiches. Money was tight, and I borrowed more from my parents, leaning heavily on the generosity of friends. It wasn't easy to ask for help. I didn't want to be more of a burden than I already was, but I had no other choice.

By the end of June, Bordeaux was getting quite warm. I either walked or took the bus to and from the hospital, where the lack of air conditioning made the heat even more oppressive. The hospital wasn't very clean either, but I kept holding on to the hope that Brian would get better and we'd be able to go home soon.

In his private room, I spent most of my time sitting beside him. Brian seemed to be improving—he was eating more, talking more, and seemed genuinely happy to listen to music or hear updates about Wimbledon. One of the doctors was a tennis fan, and our conversations occasionally turned to matches instead of tests and treatments, which was a welcome distraction. But on Saturday, June 23rd, Brian had a rough night and barely slept. By the next day, he was exhausted, didn't talk much, and was uncomfortable with his catheter. I felt helpless but tried to do what I could—washing him, combing his hair, clipping his fingernails, and asking the nurse to shower him. By Sunday evening, things hadn't improved. Brian was utterly drained, and I was sinking into despair. I noticed his IV bag was empty and had to call the nurse to replace it. I felt frustrated, like the nurses weren't paying close enough attention to him. I wanted so badly to get him out of that hospital bed and try something—anything else.

Over the next few days, Brian's condition seemed to improve. He ate well, talked more, and even complained about pain on the left side of his body. The doctors ran additional tests, including an endoscopic exam, which revealed an ulcer causing him discomfort. They prescribed medication, and it seemed to help. For short periods, he was able to sit in a chair beside his bed, giving me hope that he was on the mend.

After his long naps, Brian would wake up with bursts of energy and alertness. During these moments, he was talkative and affectionate, telling me how much he loved me. But there were troubling signs too—he couldn't remember simple things like his birthday or mine. Those gaps in his memory terrified me, even as I clung to the hope his overall progress suggested.

The doctors discontinued the antiviral treatment after eight days and removed his IV, believing the immediate infection was under control. Meanwhile, the American Consulate and others shared stories about cases where individuals had contracted an infection leading to encephalitis, which is sometimes referred to as "sleeping sickness." In those cases, patients had slept deeply for about a week and then recovered. But Brian's case was far more complicated. The cause of his encephalitis remained a mystery, and it was clearly more severe than the anecdotes I had heard. The uncertainty of it all left me deeply unsettled.

By June 26th, Brian's condition began to deteriorate rapidly. He became almost unrecognizable, moving through the day like a shadow of himself. He ate painfully slowly, slept most of the time, and seemed disconnected when he was awake. His speech became infrequent, though there were still occasional glimmers of the man I knew. During those brief moments, he would hug me, tell me he loved me, and even greet the nurses with a soft "Bonjour."

A specialist was brought in to review Brian's case, which gave me a sliver of hope. Unfortunately, the specialist shared very little information with me, leaving me in the dark. Desperate for answers, I reached out to the consulate for an interpreter, hoping they could help me navigate the language barrier. Even with their assistance, so many of my questions remained unanswered, and I was left feeling helpless and overwhelmed.

The days dragged on endlessly as I stayed with Linda and Olivier, longing to be home and for life to return to normal. I struggled to accept the reality of what was happening—it felt surreal, almost impossible to believe. My thoughts revolved entirely around Brian and waiting for him to get better. Nothing else mattered.

I stayed in touch with my parents and Brian's parents regularly, sharing updates and seeking comfort in their voices. The saxophonists occasionally came by to visit, but the conversations were difficult. Communication was a challenge, and the silence between us was heavy with unspoken fears. No one knew what to say, and what could anyone say in a situation like this? It was an awkward and helpless feeling for everyone.

On June 29th, I arrived at the hospital to find the doctor and nurses gathered around Brian. His fever had spiked, and he was unresponsive. They quickly moved him to a different room on the third floor. He spent most of the time sleeping, while I spent most of it crying. I was overwhelmed with confusion and fear. Just when I thought he was improving, everything took a turn for the worse. The language and cultural barriers made everything harder. No one explained what was happening or why Brian's condition had deteriorated so suddenly. Seeing his eyes rolling back in his head was terrifying. It filled me with a deep sense of dread. Over the next few days, they ran more tests, including numerous spinal taps and blood draws, but I still didn't have any answers.

One day, I arrived at the hospital to find Brian's room empty. Panic overtook me, and I was hysterical, convinced he had died. Frantically, I ran down the hallway to the nurses' station, shouting, "Where's Brian? Where's my husband?" A nurse finally approached and told me she would take me to him, but she didn't explain anything or tell me what was wrong. Before I could see him, I had to put on a long blue gown, slippers over my shoes, and a cap over my hair. Then she led me to a glass cubicle in the ICU. There, Brian lay hooked up to oxygen, an IV, and multiple monitors. Wires and tubes surrounded him, and he was completely unresponsive. The sight was almost too much to bear. How had it come to this? It felt like I was trapped in a nightmare, one I couldn't wake up from.

Chapter Five
The Long Road Home

Some of Brian's saxophone classmates continued to visit, helping me with small translations when they could. I reached out to the American Consulate for assistance with interpreting medical information, applied for government aid to help cover Brian's hospital expenses, and submitted paperwork to extend our stay in the country. Part of the communication issues stemmed from the fact that the hospital didn't realize I was Brian's wife, likely because I was so young, just 20 years old.

I spent countless hours at the hospital's entryway payphone, calling my family in America and asking them to research Brian's symptoms and treatments. I was beginning to doubt whether he was receiving the proper care, especially since he was worsening instead of improving. Through their research, I learned that in the U.S., the antiviral medication Acyclovir was typically administered for 21 days, much longer than the eight days Brian had been given. Determined to advocate for Brian, I arranged another meeting with the neurologist to discuss his treatment plan. I begged the doctor to restart the medication, explaining that Brian had shown noticeable progress while on it and a sharp decline when it was discontinued. During the meeting, the doctor revealed that Brian had suffered a seizure. To minimize further brain damage and reduce the risk of swelling, they had induced a coma.

Brian had been in the hospital for over four weeks, confined to a bed and unable to move. During that time, he received no physical therapy or any form of rehabilitation. He could no longer eat on his own and was fed through a tube. His body began to curl into a fetal position, and his hands were swollen from clenching into tight fists. To prevent his fingernails from digging into his palms, I placed rolled-up washcloths in his hands. I did everything I could to care for him. I massaged his feet and legs following the healing techniques my sister had researched, which included acupressure and reflexology. I read to him so he could hear my voice, placed cool washcloths on his forehead to ease his fever, and played his favorite music in his ear. I read letters from home and told him—again and again—how much I loved him and how desperately I needed him to get better. Every moment, I poured my heart into comforting him in any way I could.

Those weeks while Brian was in the ICU were grueling and unbearable. To make matters worse, Bordeaux was in the grip of a heat wave, and the hospital had no air conditioning. Brian was already burning up with a fever, and their solution to keep him cool was to let him lie there completely uncovered. When I walked in and saw him like that, I was furious and immediately made it clear that it was unacceptable. My frustration needed no translation. After that, they brought in a device to prop the sheet above his lower body, offering him at least some dignity.

My patience and hope were wearing thin. The only time I found any semblance of peace was when I was near him. I also needed to find another place to stay. Staying at Linda and Olivier's was becoming difficult, especially since I was often sleepwalking at night, and they were preparing for the arrival of their second child. The Bordeaux-Los Angeles Club once again became my lifeline. Two American couples, Gail and Loren, and Cindy and Mark, opened their homes and their hearts to me for extended periods. They fed me, gave me a place to stay, and provided a sense of security when I wasn't at Brian's side. I will never forget their kindness and generosity. I had no money, yet they set a place for me at their dinner tables every night, offered me a room to sleep in, gave me rides to and from the hospital, and wrapped me in their support and compassion. Their incredible acts of kindness astounded me, reminding me that even in the darkest times, someone was looking out for me. I can't imagine how I would have survived without their selflessness. I don't know if I can ever truly repay them, but the best way I can think of is to pass on their generosity and to be as kind and giving to someone else in desperate need, just as they were to me.

The first glimmer of hope came in the form of a smile from my beloved. The nurse was there to witness it, so I knew I wasn't imagining it. There had been moments when Brian opened his eyes, but I couldn't tell if he was truly seeing me. But on July 15th, everything changed. When I walked into the room, he smiled...*really* smiled. It was the first time in weeks, and my heart soared. Brian was waking up. His fever was finally starting to subside, and with that smile, hope flooded back into my soul.

Brian's smile was all I could talk about. It was the only thing on my mind. I went straight to my dear friend Mme. Cazemajou to share the news and stay for dinner. Countless times, I found myself at her doorstep, seeking comfort, and she consistently provided it without hesitation. I'm not sure if she or my other friends truly understood just how much they meant to me. They were my lifeline, holding me up so I could stay strong for Brian. Without their friendship and unwavering generosity, I honestly don't know how I would have managed.

Brian was surrounded by tubes and machines, and every time I walked into his room, I braced myself for the sight of something new. One day, I was startled to see yet another device, only to laugh when I realized it was a pair of headphones. The nurses had noticed me sharing my headphones with Brian to play music and thoughtfully brought in their own set to play jazz for him. The music made a difference. Hour after hour in that stifling hospital room, with only the hum of machines to break the silence, Brian needed stimulation. I worked with him to blink once for "yes" and twice for "no," teaching him small ways to communicate. Some days he was more alert than others. Often, he grimaced as if he were in pain, but it was clear that he was most responsive when I was by his side. He reached out to hold my hand, rubbing my palm gently—a gesture that filled me with hope.

During a meeting with the doctor, I finally received some encouraging news. He confirmed that Brian's condition was caused by a virus and assured me he would make a full recovery. He also explained that Brian had experienced an epileptic seizure but promised to keep me better informed moving forward. Those moments of progress, no matter how small, felt monumental and gave me the strength to keep going.

The days felt endlessly long as Brian remained in the ICU for weeks. Visiting hours were limited to less than five hours, but I stayed by his side as long as I could until the nurses gently asked me to leave each day. During those precious hours, I read him letters from home, massaged his hands, hugged and kissed him, and did everything I could to keep him stimulated. Most of the time, though, I was so drained from anxiety and sleepless nights that I would sit beside him with my head resting on his chest, holding his hand.

I couldn't stop worrying about how frail he had become. It was heartbreaking to see him so thin and weak, and I longed more than anything for him to recover. Every small sign of progress felt monumental. He could lift his eyebrows, reach for me, smile, scratch his head, or even grimace if he didn't like the taste of something. Slowly, we began introducing soft foods, such as yogurt and pudding. Even sitting upright in a chair for short periods of time left him completely exhausted, but it was a step forward. Brian's progress was slow, but the signs of recovery were undeniable. He was eventually moved out of the ICU and into a private room, which allowed me to spend more time with him. However, he suffered a setback with another high fever, followed by several days of unresponsive sleep. During this time, the doctors discontinued one of his antibiotics and questioned whether the encephalitis was viral or bacterial in origin. He underwent countless tests and many of which I'll never fully understand, and was given a variety of medications, some of which caused allergic reactions. At times, it felt as though Brian was becoming more of a research subject than a patient, which was both frustrating and terrifying.

The aftermath of encephalitis and weeks of immobility took a heavy toll on his body. He developed a blood clot in his bladder, his muscles and tendons began to contract, he endured severe stomach pain from an ulcer, and he suffered from debilitating constipation. I did my best to care for him, keeping him as clean and comfortable as possible. I clipped his nails, trimmed his hair, and persistently begged the nurses to give him a proper shower. Most days followed a monotonous routine: bed baths, feeding him meals, reading aloud, napping by his side, feeding him dinner, and finally heading home while he stayed in his hospital bed. But by the end of August, there was a breakthrough. I managed to get Brian into a wheelchair and took him outside for the first time since he fell ill in early June. Feeling the fresh air and warm sunlight on his skin seemed to lift his spirits, even if only a little. With the wheelchair, I was able to take him downstairs to the payphone. Holding the receiver close to his ear, I let him listen to the familiar voices of Susan and my mom. Hearing their love and encouragement over the line brought something no medicine could—comfort, hope, and healing for his soul.

We spent our first wedding anniversary in circumstances I could never have imagined. By September, I had another meeting with the doctor, who informed me that Brian had suffered significant brain damage. He couldn't predict how much Brian would recover. To make matters worse, the French authorities were unwilling to pay for extended rehabilitation, meaning we would have to leave after three months. I had been praying for a way to get Brian home, but the logistics seemed impossible. Flying with Brian in a coma, with no money and expired insurance, felt insurmountable. We were entirely at the mercy of the French medical system. Brian's family was desperately exploring options to bring him back to the U.S. for further treatment.

Not long after, Brian was transferred to a rehabilitation hospital across the street. His new roommate was a young boy who had suffered brain damage in a motorcycle accident. The boy had severe behavioral problems and short-term memory loss, making the environment even more challenging to endure. Despite being in a rehab center, Brian received very little actual therapy. Most of his days were spent lying in bed, staring at the ceiling. He sank into depression, rarely smiled, and often refused to eat. It broke my heart to see him like that. I sometimes had to resort to feeding him with a syringe or buying junk food to coax him to eat. Many times, I called my dear friends Gail and Loren to help me feed him. Those were some of the hardest days. One moment stands out vividly. Brian was wearing headphones, listening to Louis Armstrong's "What a Wonderful World." When the song began, tears streamed down his face, and he pulled the headphones off. The sight of him crying crushed me; I thought my heart might break completely. In those moments of despair, I would wheel him outside to escape the oppressive sadness of his hospital room. The fresh air and sunshine gave us at least a slight reprieve, a moment of privacy and solace.

What I longed for most was to hear Brian's voice again. I wanted him to talk, to laugh, to be himself again. Despite his silence and immobility, I could still see the essence of him in his eyes. While his roommate had a blank, empty stare, Brian's eyes remained a window to his soul. The sparkle, the life, the "Brian-ness" that made him who he was; it was still there. Even though he couldn't respond as he once did, I never doubted that Brian was listening. His presence was still palpable to me in the way he looked at me. I clung to that connection, finding strength in the love I saw in his eyes. That light, that essence of him, kept me going.

Gail and Loren were always there to help me feed Brian, especially on days when I couldn't manage alone. Sometimes he refused to eat, and his frail, thin frame was heartbreaking to see. In my moments of despair, I would call them in tears, and they would come without hesitation. Cindy, with her naturally cheerful and lighthearted personality, also came by often. She had a remarkable gift for making us laugh, even during the darkest times. These friends became my lifeline. Their kindness and support carried me through when I felt like I couldn't go on. The connections I made through the Bordeaux/Los Angeles Club—Gail, Loren, Cindy, Mark, Jill, Peter, Linda, Olivier, and Madame Cazemajou—were nothing short of a blessing. Their generosity and compassion continue to inspire me to this day, and I will be forever indebted to them. Their kindness is something I will never forget.

Back home, Brian's family was organizing a fundraiser to raise the $10,000 needed to fly him back to the States. Meanwhile, my family was researching hospitals and exploring financial assistance options, such as Medicaid and Welfare. Brian's father, a veteran and Air Force employee, tried to arrange for a military flight from Germany to stop and pick up Brian. My own father, a former Marine, also did everything he could to support the effort. One day, I was on a speakerphone call with the American Consulate, discussing the possibility of securing a military transport. Unfortunately, during the call, someone forgot to put me on hold or mute. To my horror, I overheard high-ranking officials laughing at my plea for help. It was deeply insulting and heartbreaking to realize that anyone could find humor in my desperate attempt to save the man I loved. There was nothing remotely funny about the situation, and their laughter felt like a cruel betrayal during one of the darkest moments of my life.

The days dragged on, each one feeling slower than the last. Many were filled with a monotonous sadness. I spent most of my time with Brian, helping him with simple tasks, such as feeding himself, playing music for him, encouraging any form of communication, and reading aloud. Though he didn't speak, there were moments when he surprised me and reminded me of the depth of his love. One day, as we sat at a table, I was helping him practice picking up peanuts to feed himself. Slowly, he picked them up one by one—not to eat, but to place them in front of me. I was overwhelmed with emotion and began to cry. Even now, that memory brings me to tears. In that small but profound gesture, I felt his love for me—pure, strong, and undeniable.

There were countless phone calls and letters exchanged between our families as we tried to coordinate Brian's journey home. The process was incredibly complex and often frustrating. It felt like every step forward was met with another obstacle, making an already difficult situation even more challenging.

There was so little I could do, so I had to trust our families to take charge. The pressure from the French authorities to take Brian home was mounting, and the hospital bill had grown astronomically. American Airlines refused to fly him, citing liability concerns, and without insurance, American hospitals didn't want to admit him. Every obstacle seemed to boil down to money. No one wanted to foot the bill. I didn't have a cent to my name, but I didn't care about the cost. How could anyone reduce Brian's life to a question of dollars and cents? The love of my life was lying helpless in a hospital bed, unable to move or speak. How could people even discuss money in the face of this? It broke my heart to see how quickly the world turned its back. Not long ago, everyone wanted to be around him; he was the golden boy, singing jingles for radio commercials, performing at events, loved and admired by so many. But now, when he needed help the most, those same people had disappeared. What is the true cost of a human life? And what would you do if it were someone you loved in that hospital bed?

After what felt like an eternity, the arrangements were finally settled. Air France agreed to fly Brian from Bordeaux to New York with a French doctor familiar with his case serving as the attending physician, as no American doctor was willing to make the trip. Our journey included an overnight layover in New York before continuing to Minneapolis and then Fargo, North Dakota. During our stop in New York, Brian had to be examined by an American doctor as part of the travel requirements.

Suddenly, everything started moving quickly. My bags were packed; they never truly were unpacked. I was almost giddy with anticipation, eager to see my family and return to America where I could speak English and feel at home again. It felt like everything was going to get better. But saying goodbye to my friends was heart-wrenching.

My dear friend, Mme. Cazemajou took me out for a farewell lunch. She had been a source of constant inspiration and comfort, and I struggled to find the right words as we sat in her car at the bus stop. Instead, there were only tears as we hugged goodbye. When my bus pulled up, I stepped out of the car, but she called me back. "Pat," she said, and handed me an envelope before driving away. She knew the only way I would accept money from her was if I couldn't refuse it. Inside the envelope was a beautifully written note, full of love and care. Her words and generosity overwhelmed me. After everything she had already done for me, she gave me money, saying I would need it. I will never forget her kindness, never.

October 20th was the day of our long-awaited flight home. Loren kindly drove me to the hospital to help Brian prepare for the journey. Together, we got him ready, and I rode in the ambulance with him to the airport. Brian was on a stretcher, frail but holding on, as we embarked on this critical step toward recovery. At the airport, however, an unexpected issue arose. The French authorities decided to pull me aside for questioning. In a small office, several security officers interrogated me about Brian's expired visa and my lack of proper documentation. They were fully aware of our situation—it wasn't a secret—and yet they chose this moment to make it an issue. I met their questioning gaze head-on and firmly told them that, unless they wanted to continue footing the bill for Brian's medical care, they needed to step aside and let us board the plane to leave their country. My words must have struck a chord because, without further argument, they released me and allowed us to proceed.

Outside, a group of our dear friends had gathered to bid us farewell. Their presence overwhelmed me with emotion. How could I ever thank them enough? So many people had done so much for us, and "thank you" felt woefully inadequate. Even now, after all these years, I still struggle to find the words to convey the depth of my gratitude. Each one of them remains etched in my heart, and I will never forget their kindness.

The journey home was long and exhausting. Brian was placed on a metal stretcher, precariously balanced across the tops of several seats in the smoking section of the plane. The French doctor who had agreed to accompany us sat nearby with her husband, but she didn't speak English and provided no assistance during the flight. I stayed by Brian's side, whispering reassurances to him, telling him over and over that everything was going to be okay now; we were finally going home.

Chapter Six
The Fragile Return

T he flight from Bordeaux to New York felt endless and exhausting. I was filled with a mix of anticipation and anxiety, while Brian endured the discomfort of lying on a stretcher for the entire journey. We didn't have the luxury of quiet or privacy. His stretcher was awkwardly positioned across several seats in the smoking section, adding to the discomfort. Despite these challenges, I stayed by his side, holding his hand and doing my best to reassure him that we were finally on our way home. We didn't eat or sleep, and Brian couldn't even move as we endured the stifling discomfort of cigarette smoke in the cramped smoking section. When the plane finally touched down on American soil, I felt an overwhelming sense of relief—we were home. However, the challenges weren't over. After all the passengers had deplaned, the paramedics came to transfer Brian, but the process was chaotic and poorly planned. They hadn't anticipated how to get him off the plane, and the only available exit was the cargo door, which was six feet above the ground. Watching them struggle to balance Brian on a stretcher as they lowered him was harrowing; I was terrified they might drop him.

To make matters worse, U.S. authorities required Brian to be examined by an American doctor before he could officially enter the country, which meant he wasn't allowed inside the airport. The situation was chaotic, confusing, and emotionally overwhelming. Just as I felt myself unraveling, I saw my Uncle Arthur walking toward us. The sight of a familiar, caring face broke through my despair, and I burst into tears of relief. He had come to support us, and in that moment, I finally felt like I wasn't alone. My uncle and cousin Steve stayed by my side as we followed the ambulance to Queens General Hospital's emergency room, where Brian underwent the required medical evaluation.

Two years earlier, I had spent a summer in New York, living in the suburbs and frequently taking the train into the city. But nothing in those experiences prepared me for the harsh reality of inner-city life that hit me the moment we walked into that ER. Chaos erupted instantly. The room was overcrowded, filled with noise and tension. Police officers were everywhere, blood stained the floors, and the air was thick with shouting, foul language, and an unbearable smell. It was overwhelming. Brian started to cry, and I could barely catch my breath.

A doctor quickly escorted Brian into a curtained exam area and listened to our situation. Thankfully, he understood immediately and agreed to sign the paperwork releasing Brian. He said Brian would be far better off in a hotel than enduring the night in that ER. I thanked him profusely, and as soon as they could, the paramedics transported us to a nearby hotel. While the American authorities initially wanted Brian to stay in the hospital overnight, the French doctor agreed to assist me with his care at the hotel. The relief I felt was indescribable. I don't think I could have lasted another moment in Queens General Hospital.

My uncle and cousin met us at the hotel, and once Brian was settled into bed, they gently insisted I go with them to have dinner. I didn't want to leave Brian—I knew he would be safe, but I couldn't shake the thought of him being scared. Still, they wanted to take care of me, and their kindness in being there was something I deeply appreciated.

When I returned to the hotel room, I showered and climbed into bed beside Brian. It was the first time in over five months, since May

10th, that I had been able to lie next to him outside of a hospital. He was so fragile and emaciated that I was afraid of disturbing or hurting him. But I couldn't help myself—I kissed him softly, over and over, and curled up close to him. For the first time in what felt like forever, I could simply be with him.

Our journey from New York to Fargo started early the next morning, and it wasn't without its challenges. There were issues with our tickets, the French doctor's husband's camera was stolen, and general chaos seemed to follow us. Thankfully, my uncle was there to help sort through the complications. But at that point, none of it mattered to me. I was determined to get on that plane with Brian, even if it meant using proper tickets or not. I had one goal: to get Brian to the hospital in Fargo.

The rest of the trip, however, was a much-needed improvement. We flew first class in a non-smoking cabin. Brian was placed on a stretcher with actual padding, and we had a curtain around us for privacy. The flight attendants were exceptionally kind, checking on us regularly. For the first time in a long while, I even managed to sleep a little during the flight. I sat right beside Brian the entire time, holding his hand and reassuring him that everything was going to be okay. I told him, over and over, that we were going home.

Brian's parents were waiting for us at the airport in Fargo. Once again, we were the last passengers to disembark, but this time, Brian was wheeled through the small terminal on a stretcher. He looked so frail, his body gaunt from the ordeal. No one looks their best on a stretcher, but after everything he had endured, Brian's appearance reflected the unimaginable toll this journey had taken on him. The trip from Bordeaux to Fargo felt like an eternity, and I couldn't begin to fathom how difficult it must have been for Brian. He hadn't eaten or drunk anything since we left France. As we arrived, I braced myself for a moment of shared emotion. I expected his parents to greet me with a hug, maybe tears of relief. After all, they had fought so hard for

Brian to come back to North Dakota. Out of all the hospitals and rehabilitation centers in the U.S. that we could have flown to, this was the place they wanted their son to be. I couldn't deny them that. If they wanted Brian home, home was where we would go. But the welcome I anticipated never came. There were no hugs, no warm greetings, not even an acknowledgment of my presence. Instead, Brian's mother leaned over the stretcher, looked at him, and coldly remarked, *"See? I told you he doesn't know who we are."*

Her words hit me like a slap. It was horrendous. She didn't say a single word to me, didn't even look in my direction. It was as if I didn't exist; as though I was invisible, merely an observer to this painfully surreal moment. I stood there, stunned, watching everything unfold, feeling completely erased.

When I left for Bordeaux in June, my world stopped. But now, as the ambulance drove through Fargo in mid-October, it was clear that time had marched on without us. I watched through the window as the seasons had shifted; leaves had turned, been raked, and neatly bagged. Halloween was just around the corner. Life had continued, indifferent to our struggles. Still, I held onto hope. I told myself that now that we were in America, everything would finally be okay. After all, that's what Brian's father reassured me every time we spoke on the phone. "It's okay. Everything is all taken care of," he'd say. He never shared specifics, but I trusted him. I had no choice but to.

I believed that no matter the dynamics of Brian's family in the past, an event like this could only bring people closer. If anything could summon a family's strength, dignity, and love, it was a crisis like this. But the reality was far more complicated. Moments like these can either unite a family, inspiring them to rise to the occasion, or they can expose cracks that shatter completely under the weight of it all.

We arrived at the hospital through the Emergency entrance, a stark contrast to the chaos we'd endured at Queens General. This ER was calm, clean, and seemingly empty, which was an unexpected relief. The French doctor and her husband had traveled thousands of miles to see us safely here. She carried the dossier, an enormous binder filled with every test, treatment, and medication Brian had undergone. More importantly, she carried the intimate knowledge of his condition and medical history. The hospital staff quickly wheeled Brian into an exam room for a thorough check. As we reached the door, an American doctor met us with a curt and cold demeanor. His first order was for me to stay in the hall. I was stunned. Then, to my disbelief, he turned to the French doctor and told her she was no longer needed. Her credentials, he said, weren't recognized here. The language barrier made his dismissiveness all the more brutal. She looked confused and humiliated. I stood there, stunned and speechless, before apologizing to her and thanking her for making the journey.

Though I had been disappointed in her lack of care for Brian during the trip, I knew no American doctor had even been willing to accompany us. She was the reason we were able to return home, and for that, I was grateful. She handed me the dossier, and I called her a cab to take her back to the airport. Watching her leave felt surreal, like another part of the safety net we'd relied on was suddenly gone.

I returned to the waiting room and sank into one of the cold, hard plastic chairs, my exhaustion heavy in the quiet air. When the American doctor finally emerged, he delivered his diagnosis with an infuriating nonchalance: "Yep, classic case of encephalitis—textbook."

I stared at him, dumbfounded. Did he think I didn't already know that? The French hospital had performed countless tests, such as spinal taps, bloodwork, and exhaustive treatments. I'd seen the evidence myself. We knew Brian had encephalitis; that wasn't why we'd come here. We'd come because we believed things would get better in America. We'd come for hope, for answers, for a plan to help Brian recover. And now, standing before me, this pompous man declared what we already knew as if he'd made some groundbreaking discovery. I couldn't believe his arrogance; his complete lack of compassion or humanity. Brian wasn't a "textbook case;" he was a 29-year-old man who had been vibrant, healthy, and talented only a few months ago. Now, he was emaciated, unable to speak or move, lying on a gurney after traveling halfway across the world for help. We came here for solutions, not to hear what we already knew.

The rage inside me was unbearable. I wanted to tear into that doctor, to make him feel even a fraction of the pain Brian had endured. What kind of person behaves with such callous indifference toward another human being? He offered no comfort or hope, only his arrogant, detached declaration of the damage already done.

The nurses wheeled Brian down the hall to his room, and I immediately got up to follow. They explained that the most critical thing for him right now was to rest and receive IV fluids because he was severely dehydrated. Suddenly, their attention shifted to me. Everyone insisted I leave the hospital to get some rest myself. I'll never forget their words, and I'll never stop regretting listening to them. To this day, the thought of leaving him eats away at me with a regret so profound it feels like a weight I'll carry forever. I know I needed rest. I know I needed to eat. I understood it then, and I understand it now. But I shouldn't have left. I should have stayed by Brian's side. His family was downstairs in the waiting room, and I told them he needed quiet and rest. Brian's aunt kindly invited me to her home for the night, but I was so exhausted and overwhelmed that I didn't know what to do. I'd never met her before; I had no money, not even a single American penny, and I felt completely disoriented. My family wasn't arriving until the next day, and I didn't even know where I was in relation to anything.

In my confusion, I ended up asking Brian's parents if I could stay at their house for the night. They hadn't offered or invited me; I had to muster the courage to ask. Looking back, I wish with all my heart that I'd borrowed money or found a way to stay in the hotel across the street from the hospital. Why didn't I think of that? Why didn't I insist on staying close to Brian? Why didn't I trust my instincts? These questions haunt me to this day.

I told Brian I'd be back in the morning. He looked so exhausted, so fragile and thin. I could only imagine how scared and confused he must have been—I certainly was. It sounds strange, but I'd say that even being back in America felt foreign. After so many months in France, it was almost surreal to understand the background chatter and speak to the nurses without a language barrier. I kissed Brian over and over, whispering how much I loved him before I left.

I don't even remember the drive to Brian's parents' house. I must have fallen asleep. I desperately needed a shower and a bed, and I kept telling myself it would all be okay because my parents were arriving the next day. That thought was the only thing keeping me going. Brian's younger sister wasn't home that night, so I stayed in her room, in her bed. From the moment I arrived, I knew it was a mistake. For all the times Brian's dad assured me that everything was "taken care of," it was painfully clear that no one had given a single thought to where I would stay or what would happen next. I felt like an afterthought.

The next morning, no one seemed to be in any hurry to leave for the hospital. I was overwhelmed with panic from being away from Brian and desperate to get back to him. I hadn't slept much, couldn't eat, and was still wearing the same worn-out clothes I'd had since June. Nothing about staying there felt right. Finally, we left for the hospital. It was a 40-minute drive that felt like an eternity. Every second away from Brian was unbearable, and all I could think about was getting back to his side.

The primary focus that morning was to give Brian a much-needed shower. In France, he'd only ever had bed baths, except for the few rare times I managed to convince the nurses to let him shower. The nurses carefully transferred him onto a shower chair, and we wheeled him down the corridor. When they undressed him, it was the first time I had seen Brian fully naked in months, and I couldn't hold back my tears. He was so frail, so painfully thin. My beautiful husband, who once stood six feet tall, now weighed only 110 pounds. Seeing him like that was heartbreaking. The nurses gently scrubbed him clean, giving him the care and attention he desperately needed. Afterward, Brian was moved to a new room equipped with an air mattress to help treat a pressure sore on his lower spine. The nurses took the time to explain to me just how severe bedsores could be. When someone is bedridden or unable to move for long periods, the constant pressure on specific areas of the body cuts off circulation. This causes the tissue to break down and die. What's even more horrifying is that the damage often starts deep near the bone and only becomes visible at the surface once the sore has progressed significantly. By then, it can be a massive, open wound—one that's not only painful but potentially life-threatening due to the risk of infection.

The healing process for a pressure sore depends on several factors: proper nutrition, good circulation, frequent repositioning, cleanliness, and sometimes just sheer luck. Brian's new air mattress was designed with multiple chambers that inflated and deflated in a cycle, ensuring no one part of his body bore the brunt of the pressure for too long. In addition to the mattress, the nurses implemented a routine of turning him every two hours and eventually getting him into a chair to relieve pressure and promote healing. This marked the beginning of my education in how to care for him. I quickly learned that turning someone in bed wasn't as simple as it seemed. It could be dangerous if not done correctly. The nurses taught me some crucial techniques. First, always raise the bed rails to prevent falls and provide reassurance for the patient. For someone like Brian, who couldn't catch himself, the fear of falling during a turn was immense. I also learned that accidents in hospitals and nursing homes are far too common. Patients often fall off beds during poorly executed turns. Watching the nurses work with such care and precision taught me the importance of these safeguards. Every movement mattered, and every precaution was vital to keeping Brian safe.

My parents and Susan arrived the next afternoon, and I had never been so relieved to see anyone in my entire life. I desperately needed someone to lean on, and when they walked in, all the emotions I'd been holding back came pouring out. I broke down.

Brian was just as happy to see them as I was. I could see the relief on his face, and it was like a weight had lifted for both of us. He even smiled, something I hadn't seen in so long. To my joy, his appetite started to return as well. Someone brought him candy corn and little pumpkin-shaped candies, two of his favorites. Watching him willingly open his mouth to eat was incredible. It felt like a small victory, a glimmer of hope. We happily fed him candy after candy, thrilled that he wanted to eat, and encouraged every bite he took. For the first time in what felt like ages, I felt a sense of relief. I even felt hopeful.

The next few nights, I stayed with my parents in a motel across the street from the hospital. Those days were long and exhausting, but I spent much of the time tackling the mountain of paperwork needed to ensure Brian received the care he so desperately needed. I filled out applications for Social Security, Medicaid, and food stamps, as well as paperwork for several long-term rehabilitation centers that specialized in brain injuries. Although the waiting lists for those facilities were long, at least I managed to get Brian's name on them. It wasn't a perfect solution, but it was a step in the right direction, and that gave me a small sense of progress in an otherwise overwhelming situation.

One of the requirements for receiving food stamps and government assistance was that I had to find a job. Thankfully, I found a position at the hospital's daycare center, which was within walking distance. Without a car and knowing no one besides Brian's family, who never offered me so much as a ride, I had no other options. The daycare staff turned out to be kind and welcoming. While my heart was always with Brian, and I hated being away from him, caring for the younger children sometimes provided a much-needed distraction from the weight of my own reality. Their laughter and innocence brought brief moments of light into my otherwise difficult days. I also made some wonderful friends there. Many people opened their hearts and homes to me, offering kindness and support when I needed it most. It was a reminder that even in the darkest times, compassion can make all the difference.

My parents were a tremendous help during their first few days in town. We managed to find an apartment about ten blocks from the hospital, which was a huge relief. There was no lease to sign, and it was conveniently located near a grocery store within walking distance. I also discovered I had a cousin, Ted, living nearby with his family in Moorhead, Minnesota, the sister city to Fargo. Slowly, things were beginning to fall into place.

Although my dad had to return to work, my mom or Susan stayed with me most of the time, offering the support I desperately needed. Within a week, Brian was transferred to the rehabilitation floor of the hospital, which turned out to be exceptional.

My sisters, Liz and Georgia, came to visit us during this time, bringing much-needed laughter and encouragement. Their presence reminded me that even in the midst of challenges, the love and support of family can make all the difference.

Everything was moving so quickly, and I was utterly exhausted. Brian must have been even more so. Yet, the medical team explained that his best chance at recovery relied on engaging him in physical, occupational, speech, and recreational therapy as soon as possible.

The more stimulation he received, the better his chances. Their encouragement gave me hope, and I remained optimistic.

Brian had his own room, spacious and thoughtfully arranged, with a roll-in shower for accessibility and a window by his bed that offered a view of the outside world. My sisters and I decorated the walls with the many cards and banners people sent, filling the space with reminders of how much Brian was cared for. His former students were incredibly kind, sending heartfelt notes filled with thoughts and prayers for his recovery.

Brian had many visitors, too. He had grown up, attended college, and taught nearby, so friends, classmates, and former students often stopped by to remind him how much he was loved. It was clear how deeply he had touched their lives; he was truly popular. I knew it was hard for them to see Brian in such a vulnerable state, just as it was hard for him to be seen that way. Those visits carried a mix of emotions, gratitude, awkwardness, and sometimes heartache. For me, it was occasionally uncomfortable not knowing who these visitors were, but I deeply appreciated their kindness and the effort they made to show Brian he wasn't alone.

The goal in rehab was to help Brian regain as much independence as possible in meeting his basic needs. Every day, we worked alongside him to assist with daily tasks like showering, dressing, brushing his teeth, combing his hair, shaving, eating, and attending therapy sessions. His schedule was demanding, but the nurses were incredibly patient and knowledgeable.

They not only guided Brian step-by-step through each activity but also took the time to teach me how and why these tasks were done in a particular way. I didn't just observe his therapy sessions. I took an active role in his recovery. I was determined to learn everything I could about his care. I watched the therapists and nurses closely, and with their guidance, I practiced each skill until I could do it myself. I learned how to pivot and transfer Brian from the therapy mat to his wheelchair. I helped him hold his fork and encouraged him to feed himself. I understood the critical importance of range-of-motion exercises.

The months Brian spent immobilized in France had taken a devastating toll. His muscles had atrophied, his tendons had shortened, and his body instinctively curled into a fetal position. Preventing further deterioration required constant effort. Every muscle, every joint, from his fingers to his toes, needed attention. It was an uphill battle, but one I was committed to fighting alongside him.

By this point, Brian was eating solid food without difficulty. He had no trouble chewing or swallowing and drank using a straw. I would feed him and hold the straw to his lips. While he could move his arms, he wasn't yet able to make deliberate, purposeful movements, aside from occasionally rubbing his head or eyes. We worked on small tasks, like holding a fork or his comb, but he wasn't able to operate things like the hospital bed controls or the TV remote. He made eye contact and followed me with his gaze, but he couldn't speak or form words with his lips. However, he did smile when he was happy, which always brought me joy. Although Brian didn't move his legs, he had full sensation throughout his body. He wasn't paralyzed; his immobility was a result of the brain damage affecting his motor functions rather than his nervous system.

It was all too much for Brian. In the third week of our stay, he suffered a significant setback. To this day, I'm not entirely sure what happened, but I suspect he had a seizure or possibly a minor stroke. For several days, his eyes wouldn't focus and would dart uncontrollably from side to side. He slept almost constantly and stopped eating altogether. Although the medical team ran some tests, they didn't uncover anything conclusive. Frustratingly, they had ignored the medical records from Bordeaux, so there was no way to compare the results of an MRI or EEG to previous scans. I knew deep in my heart that something serious had occurred, but everyone seemed determined to downplay it.

I had a unique bond with Brian, and I noticed subtle changes that others often missed. But this time, the change was impossible to ignore. After a few days of rest and the insertion of a feeding tube through his nose, we essentially had to start over. Brian was no longer himself. His face was expressionless, his eyes empty, and he seemed like a shell of the person he had been. He was still painfully thin, and now, his spirit seemed diminished as well.

Chapter Seven
Love Will Carry Us

B rian faced a setback, and we had to start over. There was no other choice—we began again. I was determined to hear his voice, to see him up and walking, and I was willing to do whatever it took to make that happen. So we rebuilt, step by step, with each day dedicated to Brian's recovery.

Our lives became structured out of necessity. Each morning, I woke early, took a shower, and had breakfast before walking to the hospital. I usually arrived in time to feed Brian his breakfast and help him get dressed. My parents helped me shop for new clothes, and we threw out the ones we'd worn in France. I couldn't bear to look at them anymore—those clothes had carried the weight of thirteen months of struggle.

With winter settling in, Fargo was bitterly cold. Brian wore soft, comfortable clothes, mostly sweatpants and turtlenecks, to make therapy sessions easier. Dressing him in regular clothes wasn't just practical; it helped restore a sense of dignity and routine. Just like how you feel better when you shower and get out of pajamas, this was an essential part of his rehabilitation.

The nurses who cared for Brian were incredible. They not only provided exceptional care but also taught me everything I needed to know: the best ways to dress and undress him, brush his teeth, shave, put on compression socks, and even make his bed efficiently. Their guidance gave me confidence and a sense of control during an otherwise uncertain time.

After breakfast, medication, and getting Brian dressed, it was time for therapy. Barb, the physical therapist, was tall, strong, and incredibly skilled. She not only worked with Brian but also taught me how to care for him. She showed me how to stretch his muscles, transfer him safely from his wheelchair to the therapy mat and back, and use tools like a gait belt. Barb explained every move: where to place my hands, how to position his limbs, and even how to protect my own body from strain. She constantly communicated with Brian, letting him know what to expect, even when something might be uncomfortable. She was amazing, and every session with her was invaluable. I learned so much under her guidance.

Brian also attended occupational therapy, where the focus was on helping him relearn basic self-care skills. I was his cheerleader, encouraging him with every small victory. He did exceptionally well feeding himself, particularly with finger foods.

In speech therapy, the goal was communication in any way possible. We used flashcards with simple "yes" or "no" responses, encouraging Brian to look at the word that matched his answer. We introduced a switchboard connected to appliances, such as a fan or TV, encouraging him to tap the switch to turn them on or off. We tried everything to stimulate his voice—singing, playing music, and using creative methods to draw out even the smallest vocalizations. Progress was inconsistent. Brian was alert and aware, but there was no predictable pattern to his responses. His eyes told me he was present, fully there, but he couldn't find the words. It was heartbreaking yet hopeful; a reminder that his journey was ongoing, and I was there to support him every step of the way.

Therapy sessions were exhausting, and Brian needed naps to recover his energy. His appetite remained strong, and nutrition was just as vital as therapy. If he opened his mouth, I made sure he ate. On weekends, a therapist would visit his room a couple of times a day to guide him through range-of-motion exercises. Otherwise, weekends were for rest and occasional socializing.

Since Brian had grown up in the area, many people knew him and came to visit, people I'd never met, from a chapter of his life before I knew him. He was well-loved and something of a local celebrity, thanks to his remarkable talent. He had been involved in every kind of musical endeavor, from playing saxophone, singing in a barbershop quartet, performing in community theater, and even recording jingles for the radio. He'd also taught at a middle school for several years before moving to Colorado.

His former students, friends, family, and old colleagues came to the hospital to see him. While their visits were kind and well-intentioned, they were often difficult. Brian's condition was far worse than most of them had imagined. Seeing him incapacitated was shocking, and many visitors didn't know what to say. Their discomfort was palpable, and though I appreciated their care, part of me wished they hadn't come. It was hard to watch them struggle to hold back tears or fumble for words. I knew Brian wouldn't have wanted them to see him like that, either. What made it even more challenging was the constant retelling of our story. Most visitors only knew fragments of what had happened and came with endless questions. Recounting the events again and again was emotionally draining. My natural instinct was to comfort them, but I didn't have the energy for it. The weight of their sadness and confusion was too much to carry on top of everything else.

Brian's family struggled to cope with his illness, and it made communication with them very challenging for me. Even now, it's hard to talk about his family. His parents visited every weekend, but they rarely came into his room, choosing instead to sit in the lobby just outside. His sisters visited a few times, but his brother never came. He lived only two blocks from my apartment, yet I saw him just a couple of times during the two and a half months we were there. I couldn't understand their behavior—their lack of involvement, their silence, or the unspoken tension I felt from them toward me. Even now, I still don't fully understand it. Strangely, my cousin and his family, whom I had only recently met, were far more present and supportive during that time than Brian's immediate family.

In December, the hospital informed me that Brian wasn't meeting Medicaid's progress requirements for continued rehab funding. They told me he had to be moved to a nursing home. I refused. Determined to find a better option, I called a formal meeting with the hospital's social worker to discuss alternatives for more rehab. Brian was on waiting lists for extended rehab facilities in several locations, but the lists were long, and as a Medicaid patient, he wasn't a priority. It all came down to money.

My mom joined me at the meeting where they tried to persuade me that a nursing home was the best option. They emphasized it was one of the better facilities in Fargo, that he'd receive some therapy, and that I could visit him daily. But I couldn't even entertain the idea. Having worked in a nursing home during high school, I knew the reality of those places, and I was adamant that Brian would not end up there—period. The hospital administration staff was furious with me, and even my family pushed back. They insisted I had no other option, that Brian wouldn't improve, and that I couldn't possibly take care of him on my own. I told them I would take care of him myself. When they asked how, I didn't have an answer—I just knew I would. I had no idea how I was going to take care of Brian on my own. I didn't have money, a home, or even a plan, but the thought of putting my husband in a nursing home and moving on with my life felt unfathomable. He was in his twenties! I had never seen anyone under 30 in a nursing home before, and I couldn't wrap my head around the idea of leaving him there. Maybe for someone older and incapacitated, it might make sense, but Brian wasn't an elderly stranger; he was my husband. We had been married for only a year. I was truly in love with him, and I couldn't accept that this was just how things were going to be. I couldn't believe he wouldn't recover. It felt impossible to imagine a future without hope. I had never encountered anything like this before, and I couldn't give up on him.

After I refused the nursing home, the hospital gave me only a few days to discharge Brian, and it was right before Christmas. I was frantic, scrambling to figure out where we could go and how we'd make it work. The nurses, though, were incredibly supportive. They ensured I was trained in all aspects of Brian's care, which included bowel and bladder management, bathing, administering medications, and therapy. Despite the pressure, I remained firm in my decision.

My sister Georgia, who lived in Lincoln, Nebraska, stepped up. She found a rehab facility there and secured an efficiency apartment for us to rent while waiting for Brian to be admitted. My cousin Ted offered to drive us from Fargo to Lincoln. With money from a fundraiser that Brian's family had held in November, I rented a conversion van without a backseat so we could lay a mattress down for Brian during the eight-hour drive. I gathered supplies, medication, and essentials, signed paperwork releasing Brian from the hospital against their advice, and prepared to leave.

On a freezing day, just three days after Christmas, we left Fargo. My mom came along, though I wasn't sure what she thought of my decision. Brian's family was angry that I was taking him away, but they hadn't proposed any alternatives or solutions. They even made it difficult to access the fundraiser money. Still, I knew staying in North Dakota wasn't an option. There was no rehabilitation hospital, and Brian needed more care than they could offer. I was determined to do whatever it took for him, even though I felt utterly alone. It was bitter cold, I was run down and sick, and the overwhelming reality of our situation made everything feel surreal.

The drive to Lincoln was grueling. We arrived late at night in the middle of an ice storm and stayed at Georgia's house for a few days because the roads were so treacherous. She lived in the country outside of Lincoln, and she, along with her friends, Ted, and my mom, helped us get through those first few days. Ted, a true lifesaver, handled several of Brian's transfers before he had to return home to his family and job. Just before New Year's Eve 1991, we moved into our new apartment in Lincoln. It wasn't ideal, but it was a new chapter, and I was determined to make it work for Brian.

***

Our first apartment in Lincoln was a small efficiency unit. It was efficient, all right—just one room where I could do everything that needed to be done, and Brian could see me, and I could see him. We were fortunate that Georgia found it for us. The apartment was brand new, and I didn't have to commit to a long-term lease; it was rented on a month-to-month basis. Planning a year felt impossible—I didn't even know how I was going to get Brian out of bed the next morning.

The moment we moved in, the space seemed to shrink, or maybe it was all the equipment we brought in: the hospital bed, my bed, the shower chair, Brian's wheelchair, and most of our belongings. We rented the hospital bed so I could raise and lower it, making it easier to transfer Brian and care for him. From that bed, Brian could watch TV, see his reflection in the mirrored closet doors, look out the window, and, most importantly, watch me wherever I was in the room.

From the first day I saw Brian in the hospital, I noticed how his eyes always followed me. Doctors, therapists, nurses, friends, and family all commented on it. I must have been a source of comfort for him, just being there. I felt deeply flattered and humbled that I was the one Brian loved and trusted most, both before he got sick and after. He needed me more than ever, and I understood the weight of that responsibility. It was an honor, even though the enormity of it was sometimes overwhelming. But I took pride in meeting the challenges life threw at me. Caring for Brian gave my life meaning and purpose. He couldn't walk, talk, eat, or move without help, and I was the one who knew him best, loved him the most, and was willing to do whatever he needed. His eyes said everything he couldn't. In them, I saw sadness, fear, and most of all, his love for me. Imagine being in his situation, unable to express yourself any other way. I could feel how much he needed me, how deeply he trusted me. And I could feel his gratitude and love in return. Everyone around us saw it too—the way Brian's eyes conveyed so much emotion. To this day, I remain amazed at the power of love. It truly is the strongest force I know.

Before the hospital bed arrived, Brian slept on my twin mattress, which was on a platform, while I slept on the floor beside him. On the second night, he slid off the bed and, thankfully, landed on me. The sudden weight startled me awake, and I'm sure it startled him, too. I carefully slid out from under him and thoroughly checked him over to make sure he was okay. Other than being a little shaken, he was unharmed. Since I couldn't lift him back onto the bed, he spent the rest of the night on my mattress on the floor. Thankfully, the next morning was our first visit from the home health aide, who helped me lift Brian back into his wheelchair.

The first few days were a whirlwind of activity. We had meetings with the home health agency and a social worker to set up a plan for Brian's care. The home health agency interviewed us and arranged for an aide to assist a couple of times a day during the first few weeks, until I became comfortable transferring Brian from his bed to his wheelchair on my own. I also needed help getting him in and out of the bathroom, which was a standard layout with a narrow doorway, a sink, a toilet, and a tub/shower combination. To accommodate Brian's shower/commode chair, a specialized wheelchair with an open seat that could roll over a toilet, I had to remove the bathroom door from its hinges so the chair could fit through. Later, when we moved to a place with a roll-in shower, the process became much easier. But in the efficiency apartment, we had to navigate the challenges of the bathtub. The solution was a tub bench: a sturdy bench that extended across the width of the tub.

The process to get Brian into the tub was tricky. I would roll him backward over the toilet, lock the wheelchair brakes, and transfer him onto the tub bench. Then, I carefully lifted his legs over the edge of the tub while ensuring neither of us got hurt. At 6 feet tall and just 130 pounds, Brian was very thin but stiff and contracted, which made every movement a challenge. One person would support his upper body, while the other maneuvered his legs into the tub. Getting Brian out of the shower when both he and the bathroom were wet was even more challenging. I knew we needed a better setup, but for months, this was our daily struggle.

Once Brian was dried off and back in bed, I dressed him and guided him through range-of-motion exercises to keep his limbs as flexible as possible. In the beginning, a kind neighbor volunteered to stop by each evening to help me transfer Brian into bed. The physical demands of his care were immense, but I was determined. I worked hard to build both my strength and confidence, and eventually, I was able to handle all of his transfers on my own—up to 16 a day—from bed to shower chair, wheelchair to therapy mat, and everywhere in between. Caring for Brian wasn't just physically demanding; it became a test of my endurance, resilience, and unwavering commitment to his well-being.

We met with a social worker to apply for assistance. Since Brian couldn't work and I was his full-time caregiver, our financial situation was dire. Brian required 24-hour care, and there was no question—I was not going to abandon him. Once again, the only official solution presented to me was a nursing home. The social worker explained the types of assistance Brian was eligible for, but because I was physically able and not seeking employment, I didn't qualify for anything. It was infuriating. If a professional caregiver had been providing the same care I was, they would have been compensated well. But because I was his wife, my labor was dismissed as a personal duty rather than recognized as real work. My role as a caregiver was undervalued entirely by society. Then, the social worker mentioned an outrageous loophole: if I divorced Brian, I could receive financial support for his care. The suggestion was insulting. I had made a legal and moral commitment to Brian, and in the eyes of the state, to uphold my wedding vows. But what happens when keeping those vows means being unable to support ourselves?

In the wealthiest country on Earth, one that prides itself on Christian values and "family first" rhetoric, where was the safety net for people like us? Where was the support for families who fell between the cracks? Brian, as a Medicaid recipient, was treated as second-class, and I wasn't even considered worthy of food stamps or basic medical care. If policymakers actually thought it through, they'd realize that supporting me as Brian's caregiver would be far less expensive than paying for him to be institutionalized.

The social worker tried to offer a small consolation: as an "essential person" in Brian's life, I was technically eligible for reimbursement for some medical care. But there was a catch—I'd have to pay out of pocket first, submit receipts, and then wait one to three months for reimbursement. That was completely unrealistic. Healthcare requires insurance just to get in the door. If by some miracle a doctor agreed to see me without insurance, any tests or procedures would cost hundreds, if not thousands, of dollars upfront. Where was I supposed to get that kind of money? I had already cut every possible expense just to keep us afloat. "Essential person," my ass.

During our first week in Lincoln, I met with the rehabilitation hospital that would be providing Brian's outpatient therapy. The waiting list for inpatient rehab was too long, so I chose to start outpatient therapy immediately. Before beginning, Brian needed a complete evaluation from a team of specialists—speech, occupational, and physical therapists. The staff gave me a tour of the facility, including the large therapy gym, before leading me outside and across the parking lot to another building. It wasn't until we approached the door and I saw the sign that I realized where we were—an adult day care. My stomach turned. I was only 20 years old, and there was no way in hell I was putting my husband in a day care. The woman showing me around hadn't asked me what I wanted for Brian, hadn't taken the time to understand us. She just assumed. I felt insulted, furious even. When I looked inside that room, I saw people slumped in chairs, staring blankly, neglected, their dignity forgotten. Brian was 29 years old. He was my husband. He was the love of my life. As long as I had breath in my body, I would never abandon him in a place like that. That was the last time the topic was ever to be discussed. I had no idea what our life was going to look like. I didn't know what the future held. But I did know this: no matter how hard it got, no matter how many people told me I couldn't or shouldn't, no matter the cost, I was going to take care of Brian myself until death parted us.

People said I was throwing my life away. Many didn't understand. But I wasn't asking for their opinions. I don't think most people ever experience the kind of love Brian and I had. True love—the kind that doesn't waver when life gets hard—is rare. If they had known that kind of love, they wouldn't have asked why I stayed. They would have understood that there was never another choice. Did they really expect me to move on while Brian wasted away in a nursing home, suffering from bedsores and loneliness? Did they think I could find happiness without him while he sat forgotten? Brian was my happiness. He was my joy. He was my purpose now. He was the love of my life. And what in this world matters more than that?

Setting up our life was exhausting. The emotional strain of endless meetings was overwhelming, compounded by exhaustion and illness. I was running on empty. Every night, I set my alarm to wake up every two hours to turn Brian—no weekends off, no vacations, no sick days. Later, I discovered a memory foam mattress topper that provided more comfort, allowing him to stay on his right side for four hours, though his left side remained painful due to bone growth in the tissue. Even with this slight improvement, I never slept through the night again for the rest of his life. I have the lines on my face to prove it.

The nurses, aides, and my own ingenuity taught me countless tricks to make caregiving easier. One of the most valuable was using a turning sheet—a simple sheet laid across the center of the bed—to help reposition Brian. Instead of pulling directly on him, I could gather the sheet and gently slide him from one side to the other. I placed a pillow between his knees and feet to keep his spine aligned and prevent pressure sores. A rolled-up beach towel behind his back helped keep him in position. He needed to have time off his back and tailbone—a break from sitting in his wheelchair all day. Preventing pressure sores became my top priority. The thought of Brian ever having to spend another night in a hospital was unbearable. If waking up every hour was what it took to keep him safe, then that's what I would do.

As I mastered his care, I grew stronger—both physically and mentally. With time, I relied less and less on home health aides and took on more of the work myself. Every new skill I learned gave me confidence. This was my life now, and I was determined to do whatever it took to give Brian the best care possible.

Even as Brian's wife, I still needed legal documentation proving I had the authority to make medical and financial decisions on his behalf. At 20 years old, not even old enough to drink, I became his fiduciary. Standing before a judge, swearing under oath that Brian was incapacitated and unable to make decisions for himself, was excruciating. Saying those words out loud made our reality all the more devastating. I was officially appointed as Brian's conservator, though legal notices were sent to his family in case they wanted to dispute my role. I knew they wouldn't. They had made no effort to be involved in his care or his life. My responsibilities included meticulously documenting every penny Brian received or spent, as well as filing annual reports signed by a notary. But while the financial side required strict accountability, the most critical decisions—the medical ones—came with no official paperwork. Those decisions rested entirely on me.

By February, Brian was attending rehab three days a week, and those were long, exhausting days for both of us. Our mornings started early. I washed, dressed, and fed him, gave him his medications, and then we waited for the HandiVan, a specialized bus with a wheelchair lift and tie-downs. Unlike the city bus, it provided door-to-door service, but demand was so high that scheduling a ride was unpredictable. Some days, we waited hours just to be picked up. Other times, we spent what felt like an eternity driving across town to pick up other passengers before finally arriving at rehab. Sitting on a noisy diesel bus for an hour was draining, and after a full day of therapy, Brian was exhausted. I worried about pressure sores from all the time he spent in his wheelchair. The last thing I wanted after such a long day was to wait again, but that was our reality—waiting. I brought books to read and snacks to get us through, but it never made the waiting any easier. We were always waiting. Waiting for doctors, waiting for the HandiVan, waiting for Brian to get better.

Susan lived in Omaha and made the 50-minute drive each week to visit us. She took me grocery shopping while an aide stayed with Brian, but mostly, she came just to spend time with us. She and Brian shared a special bond—they had been tennis partners and both had a deep love for music. Whenever Susan walked through the door, Brian's face would light up.

Chapter Eight
Battles & Breakthroughs

J anuary was particularly tough on him. The stress of adapting to our new reality weighed heavily, and he often refused to eat. He was too thin, and the sadness in his eyes was heartbreaking. Then, one February evening, something incredible happened. Susan had come over, and while I was making spaghetti, she kept us entertained. Then, Brian laughed. A real, full-hearted laugh—the first in months. It was the most beautiful sound. He started giggling and couldn't stop. And with his lifted spirits came his appetite. Susan fed him plate after plate of spaghetti until I thought he would burst. His face and shirt were covered in sauce, but I didn't care. He was eating. He was laughing. Something shifted that night; it felt like a breakthrough. Susan and I were overwhelmed with joy, watching Brian come alive again. That night, she decided to stay over, and Brian kept giggling in his sleep. I had no idea what he was laughing at in the middle of the night, but I didn't care. I just lay there listening, soaking in the beautiful sound.

Our first appointment with the neurologist in Lincoln was the day after Brian laughed. The doctor reviewed Brian's medical history while we sat there, but there was no physical exam. Most of the necessary tests that included scans, EEGs, and other evaluations had to be scheduled after this initial consultation. However, without hesitation, the neurologist told me that Brian's laughter was due to seizure activity in his brain. He wanted Brian to have an EEG the next day at the hospital.

His words terrified me. The night before, I had been overjoyed to hear Brian laugh. I never imagined it could be a sign of something bad. I had no idea what to do. When Brian laughed again, I actually told him to stop. After months of longing to hear his voice, I was now asking him to be quiet. I felt completely distraught.

The next day, Brian underwent the EEG. The technician carefully placed dozens of tiny wires on his head, and he grew anxious, repeatedly trying to pull them out. I was just as nervous, dreading what the test might reveal. We both could've used a sedative, but only Brian got one. Once the electrodes were in place, we sat there, watching and waiting. I even made Brian laugh a few times to ensure the machine recorded his brain activity during those moments. Then we went home, and we waited. Every time Brian started to laugh, I tried to distract him. I didn't want him to have seizures. I kept waiting for the doctor's call. The hours dragged on. He never called. Two days later, I called his office. They assured me he would call me back right away. He didn't. On the third day, I called again and told the receptionist I would hold until the doctor was available. I was exhausted, frustrated, and consumed with worry. Was Brian having seizures? Was his laughter something dangerous? I needed answers. Finally, when the doctor got on the phone, he told me the EEG showed no signs of seizure activity. "Maybe he's just laughing because he's happy," he said.

I nearly screamed. How dare he make me wait four agonizing days—ninety-six hours—only to tell me something so obvious? I had spent those days suppressing Brian's laughter, fearing it was harming him, when all along, it was simply joy. After everything, I had told him to stop expressing himself. That neurologist stole that beautiful breakthrough from us. Once again, a doctor dismissed my instincts, relying instead on textbook definitions that reduced Brian to a generic case study. He couldn't fathom that Brian, despite his injury, was capable of happiness. I never wanted to see him again. But I was done holding back Brian's laughter. I was relieved he wasn't having seizures, and I wanted to hear him laugh every chance he got. I turned into a clown, doing anything and everything to make him giggle. His appetite was returning, and I made it my mission to help him gain weight. He was so thin I could see his ribs, and he needed strength to heal. I spent hours preparing well-balanced meals and snacks, determined to nourish him back to health. Laughter and good food—those were the real medicines Brian needed.

Although Brian had started eating more, he still refused to drink. Even before he got sick, he never liked water. He would sip through a straw, but in the smallest amounts. It could take him hours just to finish a couple of glasses. He was stubborn about it, too, shaking his head or turning away in refusal. But staying hydrated was crucial, mainly because of his medication and immobility. His body needed extra fluids to keep his digestive system working and to support his recovery.

I stayed busy managing all of Brian's care—taking him to therapy, waiting for the Handivan, preparing meals, and feeding him. Then, during physical therapy, he started wincing. I mentioned it to the therapist, but the next day, something even more concerning happened. He bit his hand. I was horrified. I quickly pushed his hand away, but he had bitten down hard, though not enough to break the skin. It was so strange. I kept asking him what was wrong, but of course, he couldn't tell me. I told the therapist I thought he was in pain. She dismissed my concerns, saying that many patients with head injuries bite themselves or others; it was just a behavioral issue. I disagreed. There was nothing visibly wrong, but he moaned a lot, and something in my gut told me he was trying to communicate his pain. After a couple more days of watching him bite his hand, my fear grew. I refused to believe this was just a "behavior problem."

The therapist decided to take a video of Brian biting his hand and send it to a brain injury specialist in Washington. I agreed, but honestly, I thought the whole thing was ridiculous. Still, I didn't want to stand in the way of Brian getting the care he needed. I had already learned that questioning medical professionals often led to tension. They took detailed notes of every interaction, and I knew from experience that too much disagreement would end up in Brian's chart as a negative mark against me. So, they sent the video, and we waited for a response. We didn't have to wait long for answers. The very next day, I noticed blood in Brian's urine. I panicked as I had never seen that before. I called the doctor and rushed in a sample. She diagnosed him with a severe bladder infection on the spot. He was immediately put on antibiotics and instructed to drink plenty of water.

Poor Brian. He had been trying to tell me for days that something was wrong, and I hadn't understood. I couldn't imagine how painful and uncomfortable it must have been, rolling around on the therapy mat with an infection. No wonder he moaned and bit his fingers.

A home health nurse suggested using a plastic-tipped syringe to help him drink. It wasn't as bad as it sounded—the small sips made it easier for him to swallow, and to my relief, it worked like a charm. Sometimes he chewed on the tip, but most of the time, he opened his mouth willingly.

By the next therapy session, the antibiotics had already eased his discomfort. And just like that, Brian stopped biting his hand. He never did it again. I told the therapists that the biting had been due to a bladder infection. I'm sure they felt bad about misjudging him, but they didn't acknowledge it. Instead, a few days later, the brain injury specialist from Washington sent back his assessment. According to him, Brian's behavior was "textbook" for a brain injury patient. He recommended a fitted glove to protect Brian's hand and medication to manage his anxiety. I didn't bother listening to the rest. It was absurd. Time and time again, Brian was underestimated and dismissed. But I knew better. I knew him better than anyone. And in that moment, I learned one of the most important lessons of my life—Trust my instincts, no matter what anyone else says.

In April, Brian was fitted for a new wheelchair—a significant milestone for us. His wheelchair was more than just a way to get around; it was essential to his daily life. He needed something sturdy, supportive, and comfortable enough to sit in for hours every day. A man named Dave Blaser came to the rehab center to fit Brian with a new chair, complete with custom-made seating. From the moment we met him, I knew he was different. He was incredibly kind, speaking to Brian directly and explaining every step of the process. He treated Brian with the respect and dignity he deserved—something that, sadly, wasn't always the case. I liked Dave instantly. I appreciated that he didn't just see Brian as a patient but as a person.

The fitting process was fascinating. Brian sat in a beanbag-like chair that slowly filled with air, allowing Dave to mold the seat perfectly to his body for the proper support. A cast was made from that imprint, and a custom foam cushion was explicitly designed for him. The wheelchair frame also had a tilt-in-space feature, which allowed me to easily recline Brian and relieve pressure when needed. With just a press of a pedal and a push on the handlebars, I could sit him upright again. The molded seat provided lateral support, preventing him from leaning uncomfortably. This new wheelchair was a game-changer. Brian sat better, felt more comfortable for more extended periods, and the chair was much easier for me to push and transfer him in and out of. It was a huge improvement in both of our lives.

Over the years, we made many trips to Dave's office—whether for repairs, adjustments, or ordering new equipment for Brian. No matter the reason, Dave was always incredibly helpful. He wasn't just knowledgeable; he genuinely cared. He made sure Brian had the best possible fit and equipment, always going the extra mile to get it right. What stood out most about Dave was how he treated people. While sitting in the waiting room, I watched him interact with countless patients, and he treated every single one with patience, kindness, and dignity. He took the time to get to know each person, ensuring they received exactly what they needed. I can't say enough good things about Dave. He was remarkable—one of those rare individuals who leave a lasting impact. I'm deeply grateful to have met him and for the care he showed Brian. I will never forget and appreciate him.

Not long after Brian received his new wheelchair, we were notified by the Department of Health and Human Services that they were disputing payment. A Medicaid court hearing was scheduled to determine whether the state would cover the cost, and we were summoned to meet with the judge. I was frantic. If Medicaid refused to pay, I had no way of covering the cost myself, and I was terrified they might take the wheelchair away. I didn't even know how much it cost; everything had been submitted through Medicaid. In desperation, I wrote a letter to the judge explaining our circumstances. Brian was receiving Social Security Disability and Medicaid, both of which were supposed to cover medically necessary equipment as prescribed by his physicians. What made the situation even more stressful was knowing that Dave and his company would be there. They were the only provider in town, and Dave had been extraordinary to us. The last thing I wanted was to create any tension or jeopardize our relationship. Still, I needed to make the judge understand why this wheelchair wasn't just a piece of equipment but essential to Brian's health and quality of life.

I explained that although the cost seemed high, this chair was something Brian relied on every single day. The custom cushion prevented pressure sores and ensured proper posture—both of which were critical to avoiding serious medical complications. Many disabled people end up hospitalized due to pressure sores or organ collapse caused by poor posture. Preventing these issues wasn't just medically necessary. It was also cost-effective in the long run. How could I put a price on something so vital? People spend outrageous amounts of money on cars they don't even use daily, while Brian's wheelchair was his *legs*—a part of him for the rest of his life. We had no money, no backup plan, and no other options.

We took the Handivan to the judge's office and waited. When we arrived, Dave and his company's representative were surprised to see us. They explained that it was standard for them to justify costs in Medicaid hearings, but they had *never* seen a patient summoned. When I told them about the threatening letter I received, Dave felt terrible. He knew Brian had missed a therapy session just to plead for the funding. Even the judge was surprised to see us there, admitting that it was highly unusual for a patient to be called in. I handed him my letter, then sat with Brian as the officials discussed business. Since the judge was running behind schedule, I had to reschedule our Handivan ride. When I used his phone to do so, he overheard the hassle—the hours-long wait, the lack of options, the endless complications. For the first time, he got a small glimpse into just how difficult every aspect of our life had become—transportation, medical care, essential equipment, and the emotional toll of it all.

In the end, the hearing was successful. The state agreed to cover the wheelchair, and we got to keep it. But the experience opened my eyes to the absurdities of our nation's healthcare system. Denying funding for a wheelchair, dentures, or a hospital bed is inhumane. We live in a country with cutting-edge medical advancements—innovations that can change lives—yet the very people who *need* them most are denied access simply because they can't afford them. And more often than not, they can't afford them *because* of their disability or medical condition. The whole system is backwards. And that day in court, I saw it more clearly than ever.

On top of the stress of potentially having to pay for Brian's wheelchair, we were also overwhelmed by relentless letters from the government demanding repayment for our return flight home. I wrote countless letters and made numerous calls, explaining why I simply couldn't repay them. It was incredibly stressful. I worried about what they might do—would they take away Brian's disability benefits? Would they threaten me with legal action? I had no idea, but their tone was anything but compassionate. Month after month, the letters kept coming. I responded with detailed explanations, emphasizing that Brian was completely disabled and unable to work, and that I was his full-time caregiver. I included a letter from his doctor and even sent copies of the Conservatorship papers, hoping to put an end to the harassment. Finally, after many exhausting months, they waived the bill but with one condition: Brian would never be allowed to leave the country again unless he repaid the amount in full. Fair enough. Brian wouldn't be leaving the country.

At times, everything felt like too much. The cost of simply surviving was overwhelming, and we had no financial cushion. We were utterly at the mercy of the system. More than anything, I missed Brian—my husband, my best friend. He couldn't speak, and the loneliness crept in. Our life was so far removed from what most people would call normal. The only people I knew in town were those who were paid to be part of our lives.

***

Brian attended outpatient rehab three times a week for several months, working with physical, occupational, and speech therapists. They welcomed my participation in every session, allowing me to learn the therapy techniques myself. Most of his physical therapy involved stretching and moving him as much as possible. We would transfer him onto a firm therapy mat and take each joint and limb through a full range of motion. Then, we worked on getting Brian to bear weight by kneeling or positioning him on all fours, focusing on balance and strengthening his muscles. Sometimes, we rolled him onto his stomach or sat him on a large therapy ball to help with core stability. I shared with the therapists that a nurse in France had noticed Brian relaxed in the bathtub. The thought of him being bathed in a standard tub—especially given his condition—was terrifying, but it also revealed how water helped ease his muscle tension. Although the rehab center didn't have a therapy pool, they did have a Hubbard Tank. It was a large tub designed to treat burn victims. Using a sling, we lowered Brian into the warm water, where we worked on his range of motion. The heat and buoyancy allowed him to move more freely, and he responded incredibly well to the sessions.

One of our biggest breakthroughs came when we found a way to stand Brian up again. The rehab center had a Tilt Table, a device that gradually moves from a horizontal to an upright position. Because Brian had been bedridden for so long, his muscles and tendons had shortened, making it impossible for him to fully extend his legs. To address this, he was fitted with leg braces designed to force his legs straight and stretch his muscles over time. The process was excruciating. I was instructed to lock the hinges as his legs straightened, and then we would slowly tilt him upright. The braces were harsh and unforgiving, and Brian would cry out in pain. One of the physical therapy aides would even press down on his knees to force his legs straight. I pleaded with them to stop, but they insisted it was necessary.

The first time Brian stood, I wept. Seeing my beautiful husband upright again after eight long months of lying in a hospital bed and only a few months of sitting in a wheelchair was overwhelming. But he could only tolerate standing for a few minutes before getting lightheaded. His body had forgotten what it felt like to be vertical, and we had to be cautious to prevent him from passing out. The rehab team sent the braces home with us, instructing Brian to sleep in them to keep his legs stretched overnight. But there was no way. I cried as I tried to make him wear them, apologizing over and over. He was already exhausted from the day's therapy, and he desperately needed rest. I couldn't bear to see him in more pain. I attempted to use the braces during the day, but even then, I couldn't bring myself to force him through such agony. Instead, I committed to doing extra stretches with him every night. I began a nightly ritual of massaging his feet and legs before he fell asleep—a small act of comfort in the midst of so much hardship.

After a few months, I grew physically stronger and relied on an aide less often. However, I still needed assistance with the shower transfer. It was a risky and challenging process, and I didn't want to take any chances. As I spent more time learning from the therapists, reading about different rehabilitation techniques, and applying that knowledge to our daily routines, my confidence grew. I was no longer afraid of hurting Brian. I learned to recognize what was helpful and what wasn't, and I could see that under my care, he was improving. Even Susan picked up on how to help transfer Brian, so on the days he didn't have therapy, we got him onto the floor to stretch. Those sessions were filled with laughter. We cranked up our favorite music, turned it into a game, and moved Brian's arms and legs in rhythm, making him "dance." He'd laugh so hard, and we'd all join in. It never felt like work—it felt like joy.

In the spring, Brian's therapy was reduced to twice a week. He would always need therapy to maintain his body's health, but because his progress had slowed, Medicaid was no longer willing to continue full funding. At times, the reality of our situation felt harsh, but I refused to lose hope. Brian had come so far. He was more expressive than ever, making a variety of facial expressions and sounds. He could vocalize. His voice was strong, but forming actual words still eluded him. Yet, I knew it was only a matter of time before he would speak again. His legs were less contracted, he was eating well, and he had gained weight. He looked great. Beyond managing his daily care, I also cut his hair. We both kept our short, spunky hairstyles, something I was determined to maintain. Brian had always received compliments on his good looks, both before and after his illness. And from me, he was never short on love and affection.

101

I met a lot of people at the rehab since I was always by Brian's side. Many would tell me they wished their family or friends were as devoted as I was. At the time, I couldn't understand why their loved ones weren't there for them. It took me years to fully grasp what they meant and to realize how unique our situation was. I was so immersed in caring for Brian that I lost perspective. From the inside, everything felt natural, but I had no idea how others saw me from the outside. I never stopped to consider how my presence with Brian—my love and dedication—impacted those around me.

To me, it was simple: I loved him. Of course, I wanted to be there. I still wanted to hold his hand, kiss his face, and spend every moment with him. My love for him didn't fade when he got sick—it only deepened. Because my devotion was so visible, people felt comfortable opening up to me. Some days, I felt like an accidental therapist. I didn't always want to hear other people's struggles, but I understood why they shared them with me. They saw in me someone who could relate to them. I heard heartbreaking stories—stories of neglect, abandonment, and cruelty. One woman with MS confided that her husband had started abusing her after she became incontinent. He ridiculed her, refused to share a bed with her, then eventually divorced her and took custody of their children. I was horrified. I had seen so many people left alone in nursing homes, their families unable—or unwilling—to cope. It was the complete opposite of the life I was living with Brian, and I knew, without a doubt, that it would never be our reality.

Whenever the weather allowed, I took Brian outside to wait for the Handivan. Some days, I just couldn't bear hearing another tragic story or answering endless questions about what had happened to Brian. Instead, we sat outside, and I read to him, or we went for walks. I didn't feel a strong connection to most people, and I didn't like retelling our story—I never felt like anyone truly understood. Instead, I poured my thoughts into my journal and leaned on my dear friend,

Jill. Whether she wanted them or not, I sent her long letters filled with emotion, frustration, and hope.

I tried everything I could to encourage Brian to speak again. Music had always been a huge part of his life, so I surrounded him with it. I played his favorite songs, replayed a video his students had made for him, and searched daily for new ideas and inspiration. One day, out of the blue, I got a phone call from a man named Stan. He and Brian had played together in the jazz band at UNC, and he had heard about Brian's condition. Now living in Lincoln, he wanted to stop by and see his old friend. I tried to prepare him, explaining that Brian could no longer speak, but he was undeterred. I agreed, but with one request—he had to bring his saxophone and play for Brian. Uncertain of how Brian would react, I called my sister Georgia for support. Would it lift Brian's spirits or make him withdraw into sadness? I had no way of knowing. When Stan arrived, the awkwardness was palpable. It was always that way when someone saw Brian for the first time since he got sick. No one ever knew what to say—what could they say? And Brian, of course, couldn't say anything. I wanted him back the way he had been more than anything, but I also loved him precisely as he was. I saw *my* Brian in his eyes, and I would do anything to help him regain his voice.

Stan was warm and kind, reminiscing for a few minutes about their days at UNC before finally taking out his saxophone. The moment he played his first note, something incredible happened. It was as if a switch flipped inside Brian. His face lit up with more than just a smile. I don't know how to describe it, except to say it was *extraordinary.* Georgia and I broke down in tears. Brian was *captivated.* Stan saw it too and kept playing, pouring his heart into the music. What happened in that moment was beyond words—a deep, undeniable connection between Brian's soul and the music. It was divine. Stan played until he was exhausted, then hugged us goodbye. That moment, that miracle, will stay with me for the rest of my life.

Chapter Nine
Homecoming & Hard Lessons

For years, I searched for someone who could regularly play the saxophone for Brian. I posted ads at the university, spoke with jazz band directors, and reached out to musicians, but no one came through. Music therapy wasn't recognized as a legitimate form of rehabilitation in Nebraska, meaning there was no funding for it. The irony wasn't lost on me. Brian had spent years bringing music to others, taking his bands to nursing homes and preschools to share the joy of live performance, yet I couldn't find a single person to return the favor.

In the summers, I took him to free concerts, hoping they would have the same effect, but they never quite captured the magic. Desperate to fill the void, I even tried playing his saxophone myself. I had never taken a single lesson, but I tried to make music for him. The notes were shaky, and my attempts fell short of what I wished I could give him. It was frustrating and disheartening. I wanted so badly to bring that joy back into his life.

As the years passed, I found that listening to someone else play the saxophone became too painful. It brought back too many memories—memories of the little things I hadn't even realized I would miss. I remembered the nights in Bordeaux when Brian would practice in our bedroom. Sometimes, I sat downstairs reading a book, but more often, I sat on the bed, watching him. I could still see it—his stance as he played, the way he always stood, the veins in his arms and along the side of his head swelling with effort, the intensity in his eyes, the heat radiating off his body from the sheer physicality of playing, and of course, the deep, beautiful sound he created. I missed it all. I grieved for *that* Brian—the musician. The world had lost not just his music, but his talent, his passion, and his ability to inspire others through teaching. And that loss was immeasurable.

***

We spent five long, difficult months in that tiny efficiency apartment while Brian underwent outpatient rehab. As much as I wanted him to get the care he needed, I missed my family deeply. We hadn't been home together since our wedding almost two years earlier, and the weight of that separation was heavy. I was exhausted from living in a single cramped room, and more than anything, we just needed to go home. With careful planning and the help of our loved ones, we finally made the trip back in May. While I looked forward to being home, I knew it would be bittersweet. By then, I had learned to manage all of Brian's care on my own, but Susan came along to help, making it possible for him to continue therapy. My parents rented a hospital bed so I could safely transfer him in and out on my own, and my dad made the 500-mile drive to Lincoln to pick us up—a journey he had to make both ways.

Brian and I rode in the back of his covered pickup truck, while Susan followed behind in her car. We laid down a mattress, piled on pillows and blankets, and traveled through the night, hoping Brian would sleep through the long ride. But he didn't. The hours stretched endlessly, making it feel as though we had been on the road for days.

Almost a year earlier, just before Brian got sick in June, he had written me countless letters while we were apart, filling them with dreams and plans for our future. We longed for the day we would be reunited on our love bench at the point, imagining the life we had envisioned together. I still treasure those letters.

Going home was a big deal. It wasn't the homecoming we had dreamed of, but I knew in my heart that it was exactly what we needed.

Once we made it up the driveway and settled Brian into his wheelchair, getting around the house was surprisingly easy. Our home was a ranch-style design with concrete floors, which made it effortless to wheel Brian through the rooms and onto the porch. When we built the house, my sisters and I used to roller skate through it, never imagining that those same smooth floors would one day be a blessing, making it easier for Brian to move around.

Brian and I stayed in my old bedroom—the one I had once shared with my younger sister, Liz. The room still had the built-in bunk beds from our childhood. I set up Brian's bed right next to the lower bunk, where he could see me and look out the window. We had hoped that our oversized shower would work for him, but unfortunately, it didn't. Thankfully, we had brought the shower/commode chair with us. Since it was summer, we came up with a creative solution—bathing Brian outside. It might sound ridiculous, but it worked. Bed baths never felt sufficient, and after all those months in the French hospital, where bathing was not a priority, I had promised Brian that would never happen again. My mom and Susan helped, and although we were out in the country, we still hung a sheet for privacy, keeping Brian covered to preserve his dignity. They passed me buckets of warm water while I carefully washed him in the sun-warmed corner of the front porch. We couldn't help but laugh at the absurdity of it all; what else could we do? And Brian, always a good sport, laughed right along with us.

While we were home, away from the rehab center, I made sure to keep up with Brian's exercises. In fact, I think I pushed him even harder than the therapists did. We had made so much progress in the past few months, and I refused to let it slip away. Every day, we set up a mattress on the living room floor and got to work. Susan helped me transfer Brian from his wheelchair to the floor. Getting him down was easy—lifting him back up was the real challenge. We each supported an arm and his legs, gently lowering him onto the mattress. With music playing, we turned his therapy into something fun. Each of us took hold of a limb and moved him in rhythm with the beat, making it look as if he were running or jumping. We sang, laughed, and cheered him on. Brian tried to put on a stern face, but laughter always won in the end.

Next, I rolled him onto his stomach and positioned him on a wedge for about forty minutes to stretch his legs. One of us would gently pull on the back of his heels while I used the Shiatsu technique to warm and loosen his muscles. Then came the hardest part—getting Brian onto his hands and knees for weight-bearing and balance exercises. I wrapped a gait belt around his waist and pulled him up onto his knees, standing over him to catch him if he lost his balance. His right arm was weak and slightly contracted, which made it hard for him to steady himself for long.

By the time we finished, all of us had gotten a workout. It wasn't just about keeping Brian strong—it was a way for my family to be part of his recovery. I knew they wanted to help, and participating in his therapy gave them a sense of purpose. It also gave them a way to connect with him. Sometimes people weren't sure what to say or how to interact with Brian, but stretching and moving with him allowed them to touch, hold, and be close to him in a meaningful way. I never needed an excuse—I cared for Brian as naturally as breathing. After stepping into the role of his caregiver, I became more aware of his body than I was of my own.

One of the most crucial parts of Brian's therapy was getting him to stand. At the rehab center in Lincoln, we used a tilt table to help him into an upright position, which had numerous benefits. It was good for his organs, helped his bones bear weight, and, just as significantly, lifted his spirits. Being confined to a wheelchair meant people were always looking down at him—both literally and, at times, figuratively. But Brian was a tall man, used to standing at his full height and having others look up to him. More than that, he was someone people admired, including me. He couldn't stand completely straight, but we were working toward it.

To continue his therapy, we drove to the local community hospital to use their tilt table. The physical therapist there still remembered Brian from his time teaching at the college. Most people in the area knew of him. Susan helped me transfer Brian into the front seat of the pickup while we loaded his wheelchair in the back. Driving with him in the front seat felt like such a simple thing, but it was a moment of normalcy we hadn't had in months. Just being able to ride together, stop for ice cream, or sing along to music in the car—those little everyday pleasures meant everything.

Since water therapy was so beneficial for Brian, Susan came up with the idea to try it at home. She bought an inflatable pool, larger than a kiddie pool, deep enough to lie down in. Before attempting to get Brian in, we made sure the water was warm. Out on the front porch, we carefully transferred him into the pool. I held him close, reassuring him so he wouldn't be afraid. It was both scary and exciting. He had always been afraid of the water since he couldn't swim, but the weightlessness made it easier to move his limbs.

Susan and I would try anything to get Brian to smile or laugh. We acted like fools, but we didn't care. She played the drums while I danced around the room, holding Brian's hands so he could tap the sticks against the drum. I put on his favorite music, grabbed his arms, and danced with him.

Georgia came for a couple of days and brought a basket full of puppies. We laid Brian on the mattress on the floor and placed the puppies around him. As they licked his face, he burst into uncontrollable laughter. That sound was everything.

Some of the music faculty and students from CSC visited as well. They were kind and well-meaning, but their presence was a painful reminder of all that used to be. The last time they had seen Brian was on our wedding day. Their lives had moved forward—marriages, babies, normalcy—while ours had been derailed. Their visits always left me emotionally drained. I tried so hard not to dwell on the past, to focus instead on what we still had. Every second of every day, I was acutely aware of how much Brian had lost, but I couldn't live in that grief. I had to hold on to the progress we had made. He was no longer lying in a coma in Bordeaux. He was home. He was with me. I could touch him, love him, be with him every day. That had to be enough, because the weight of everything we had lost was more than I could bear.

As if my heartache wasn't enough, I soon had to face another devastating loss. While I was at Brian's bedside in France, my family had kept something from me, not wanting to add to my burden. Around the same time Brian got sick, my dad lost his job with the railroad. He had been fighting his case in court, but he hadn't worked in months. With no income, they couldn't afford the mortgage, and they lost our home.

It wasn't just a house. My mother had designed it, and my father had built it with his own hands—every board, every nail, every brick bore his fingerprints. It was the place where Brian and I had fallen in love, where we had married. And now, it was being taken from us. My parents had a couple of months left before they had to pack up everything and move. My dad owned another house in a town two hours away, a place he used when the railroad stopped running through Chadron. But it was just a house. Our home, the one on the hill, with acres of open space, the one where we had grown up, where our roots ran deep—that was irreplaceable. Losing it felt like losing a part of myself. I thought the pain might break me.

***

Returning to Lincoln was disheartening, but we had no choice; it was our reality. Just like in Fargo, the rehab facility informed me that

Brian's funding was running out. I met with the home health agency to explore other options. I had my heart set on taking Brian to Craig Hospital in Colorado, a world-renowned facility known for its innovative rehabilitation techniques for spinal cord and brain injuries. However, a nurse also mentioned a rehab center in Kansas that specialized in brain injuries. I applied to both.

A year earlier, Brian had been applying for university teaching positions. Now, we were applying for a chance at rehab. Craig Hospital in Colorado accepted Brian for a ten-day outpatient evaluation, which Medicaid would cover, but we would have to pay for travel, lodging, and all other expenses. The rehab in Kansas, on the other hand, offered a fully covered ninety-day inpatient evaluation. I desperately wanted to take Brian to Craig, but when I asked my parents if they could help financially, they encouraged me to consider Kansas due to the cost. I felt torn. I didn't want to settle for Kansas without exploring every possible avenue for Brian's recovery. But without money or resources, I had little choice.

After intense pressure from my family and medical staff, I agreed to visit the Kansas facility. I left Brian in the care of Kristy, the only home health aide I trusted completely. She was my age and had become more like a friend. I hated the thought of leaving Brian for an entire day, but I had to. The nurse and I made the three-hour drive straight south from Lincoln, toured the facility, and drove back the same day.

The rehab in Kansas offered intensive physical, occupational, speech, and even music therapy. Depending on Brian's progress, he could stay beyond the initial ninety days. But something about the place didn't sit right with me. I didn't like it. Still, with no car, no money, and no way to get Brian to Craig, I felt out of options.

My sister Georgia drove me back to Kansas to find an apartment for the duration of Brian's stay. Once again, Kristy stayed with him, and I called multiple times to check in. They were fine, but I felt uneasy being away. Georgia and I spent the entire day searching for an apartment, but found nothing. Frustrated and exhausted, I was beginning to resent Kansas altogether.

Time had run out. Brian's rehab in Lincoln was ending, our apartment lease was up, and it was time to move him to Kansas. I planned to find housing once he was settled. The hospital had a house for patient families, similar to a Ronald McDonald House, but it was only intended for short-term stays, typically three days or less. Many patients came from far away, and most families left their loved ones in the hospital's care with infrequent visits. Some patients were there for temporary rehab, but many had suffered severe brain injuries and were there indefinitely. I hated the place the moment we arrived.

My mom and Susan came along to help with the move. Susan had to return to work, but my mom planned to stay until I found a place to live. I knew this wasn't the future Brian and I had imagined, but I had to make the best of it—for him, for us.

Our time at the so-called "rehab" in Kansas was one of the worst experiences of my life. Even now, it isn't easy to talk or write about. The nine days we spent there were pure hell. From the start, nothing felt right. I couldn't find housing, and I took it as a sign; divine intervention telling me I wasn't supposed to be there. The hospital informed me that I wasn't allowed to stay in their family house for more than three days. Buried in the fine print, they pointed out a policy requiring families to give three weeks' notice before visiting. Alarm bells went off. This was a huge red flag. But what could I do? Our apartment in Lincoln was gone, Brian's therapy there had ended, and we had no car, no money, no backup plan.

My mom stayed with us, trying to reassure me, urging me to stick it out. But I was in panic mode. The staff made it clear they didn't want me there, treating me with blatant hostility. Worse, they neglected Brian. He only received therapy if I took him myself. They didn't want me there, yet no one came to care for him, to bathe him, to take him to therapy. If I hadn't stepped in, he would have been left in bed all day, ignored. I was terrified—everything about this place was wrong, and I knew it.

I still don't know how or why we managed to last those nine days. My mom found an elderly couple down the street from the hospital who agreed to rent us a bedroom for a few days. My sister had loaned us her car, but I would rather have slept in it than stayed in that house. Most of the time, I refused to leave Brian's side. Every fiber of my being screamed at me to get out, but I didn't know how.

The staff ordered tests Brian didn't need, and when I questioned them, the mistreatment got worse. The final straw came when I decided to see what would happen if I wasn't there. I stayed in Brian's room, waiting to see if anyone would check on him. His room was at the end of the hall. I waited. And waited. No one came—not to bring him food, not to reposition him, not even to see if he was alive. Hours passed.

Then, early in the morning, a new patient arrived across the hall. They wheeled him in on a stretcher and left. No introductions, no check-ins—just left him there. I watched, horrified, as the hours passed and no one came to check on him either. It wasn't until late afternoon that a nurse finally entered his room. Seconds later, alarms blared—Code Blue. The staff swarmed his room, but it was too late. He had suffocated. That was it. I didn't need another sign. I didn't need more proof. That place was rotten to its core.

I was furious, terrified, and sick to my stomach. My instincts had been screaming at me from the start, and now I knew why. I packed Brian's things and told my mom we were leaving. She panicked, asking where we would go, but I wasn't asking—I was telling her. I didn't care if we had to sleep on the street. I would never let those people near Brian again.

When I informed the staff, I was taking Brian, they fought me on it, claiming I "couldn't" take him. Bullshit. I signed the paperwork stating I was removing him against medical advice. Medical advice? More like a fraudulent operation preying on the most vulnerable. This wasn't a rehab facility—it was a nursing home disguised as a hospital, scamming insurance companies and families out of money. Unnecessary tests, procedures, and even surgeries were performed on patients who couldn't speak for themselves. Abuse and neglect ran rampant. This place wasn't just bad—it was evil. That was the moment I realized some people are truly evil. They weren't just incompetent. They knowingly did horrific things to innocent, helpless individuals who had no way to fight back.

I got Brian into my sister's car and drove straight to a motel in the next town. With his wheelchair in the car, there wasn't enough room for our luggage, so I had to make a second trip. I had no idea what we were going to do next, but I knew one thing. We weren't staying there another second.

Once we were safe in the motel, I called my family. I had never felt so shaken in my life. That night, I reported the facility to the Department of Health and Human Services. When I spoke to a representative, she told me they had never received a complaint before. I didn't care. "Get a pen and paper," I told her. "Start taking notes."

I don't know if my report made a difference, but I'd like to believe it did. Years later, I learned the place had finally been shut down. Other complaints followed—abuse, neglect, deaths, rapes. God only knows what else happened within those walls. I had nightmares about that place for years.

Once we settled into the motel, I called my sisters for help. Susan helped us get back to Lincoln, and Georgia let us stay with her for several days. Her house wasn't wheelchair accessible, but at that point, we were desperate. I didn't care if we had to sleep outside. I was just relieved to be out of that nightmare and as far away from that place as possible.

Susan found a ground-floor, one-bedroom apartment in Omaha that the three of us could share until we figured out a more permanent solution. The building was unique, a circular complex where all the apartments faced a central courtyard. Most of the residents were elderly, and while the landlord was understanding of our situation, the neighbors were a little too curious for comfort.

My friend and home health aide, Kristy, assisted us with the move. She drove the truck with all our belongings, including Brian's heavy medical equipment, which took up a lot of space. There was no way I could have managed without her and my sisters.

The apartment was cramped, but we made it work. Susan gave Brian and me the bedroom while she set up her own space in the living room. It wasn't big, and she had no privacy, but she never complained. The biggest challenge was the bathroom—it had a narrow doorway and a standard tub-shower, making it challenging to get Brian in and out. I reached out to a home health agency for assistance and enrolled Brian in outpatient therapy at Immanuel Hospital.

Twice a week, we took the Handivan to and from therapy, always drawing an audience. No matter what we did, I could feel the eyes on us. The residents watched us like we were a reality show playing out in real time. A few times, we even caught a woman peeking through our window to see what we were doing. It was frustrating, but also a little funny. I understood that our situation was unusual. Most people had probably never seen anything like it—but the way they stared, without ever speaking to us, made us feel like we were under a microscope. It was one of the strangest living experiences I'd ever had.

Living in Omaha with Susan was actually a lot of fun. She had an old Volkswagen Beetle, and somehow, we managed to get Brian in and out of it—though I still don't know how we pulled it off. Since his regular wheelchair was too big and didn't fold, we borrowed a collapsible one from the American Legion. Over time, we perfected the transfer process. I would stand in front of Brian, leaning him forward while Susan sat inside the car, pulling him in. It was tricky— he was tall and stiff, so we had to be careful with his head and legs while making sure the wheelchair didn't get in the way. Once he was inside, we folded up the chair, and off we went. Driving around town, listening to music, going to the mall, catching a movie, or grabbing a bite at a restaurant—it felt like we were living an everyday life again. Or at least, as normal as life could be for us.

Georgia found us an apartment in Lincoln through an organization called The League of Human Dignity, which advocates for the rights of people with disabilities. They were building a new apartment complex, and Brian and I qualified as a priority case. Our names were placed at the top of the waitlist, but we had to wait until February for it to be ready.

In the meantime, Brian was making progress in therapy. His physical therapist agreed with me that the leg braces and tilt table were outdated and unnecessarily painful. Instead, she introduced us to a much better alternative—the Easy Stand. This standing aid allowed Brian to stand without braces or discomfort. It had a hydraulic pump, knee pads, and an anti-tip frame. I would pivot-transfer him from his wheelchair to the seat, position his legs, fasten the seatbelt and chest strap, and slowly pump him into a standing position. Moving gradually was key to allowing his body to adjust and preventing him from passing out.

The Easy Stand was life-changing. Of all the therapies Brian received, this was the most effective. It was incredible to see how well his body responded to standing after spending so much time sitting or lying down. His physical therapist agreed and arranged for us to have one at home, making daily use far more practical than traveling to the hospital every day. It took a couple of months for the application to be processed, but we finally received it in February when we moved into our new apartment.

Chapter Ten
Becoming Zoe's Mama

While Brian stood in the therapy gym, we got to know others on their own rehabilitation journeys; people with head injuries, spinal cord injuries, and those recovering from surgeries. Some were in better condition than Brian, others worse, but the atmosphere was overwhelmingly positive. No matter the challenges, hope was alive and well.

Immanuel Hospital had a therapy pool, and while getting Brian dressed for therapy—then doing it all over again after the pool—was a hassle, it was absolutely worth it. The water made moving him so much easier. I didn't go in with him, but I always stood beside the pool so he could see me. It reassured him that I was there and hadn't left, which was especially important because he was afraid of water—he couldn't swim.

When our apartment in Lincoln was finally ready, Brian's formal therapy came to an end. From that point on, I became his physical, occupational, and speech therapist. It was a huge responsibility, and I wanted regular check-ups to make sure I was doing everything correctly and that Brian was making progress. Unfortunately, no such support system existed. Since Brian was on Medicaid, there was no more funding for his rehabilitation. The idea that someone in Brian's condition was "done" with therapy was absurd.

In February, we moved into our brand-new apartment with the help of my sisters and Kristy. The complex had six units, all fully wheelchair accessible, and we were the first to move in. We got the end apartment, which turned out to be the best one. The highlight? The bathroom. It was the largest bathroom I had ever seen, fully tiled with a sloped floor for a roll-in shower—no more risky transfers! I was beyond thrilled. While most 21-year-olds get excited about a new car and the freedom it brings, I felt that same kind of elation over our apartment. For the first time, I could bathe Brian safely, without assistance. We could live like normal people and use the bathroom whenever we needed. It was a huge deal.

The apartment was in a perfect location. It sat beside a busy street with a bus stop right at the corner, and Lincoln had wheelchair-accessible buses. Taking the bus was still a challenge, but at least we had the option. We were within walking distance of several grocery stores and most of our everyday shopping needs. Best of all, we were just a block away from the wheelchair supply store where Dave worked. To the north of the apartment was a quiet neighborhood with a long bike path. We could take walks for miles without worrying about curbs or traffic.

For the first time in a long time, things were finally looking up. I decorated our apartment to make it feel like home—a place where we could finally breathe again. For the first time in a long time, I felt like celebrating life. More than anything, I wanted Brian to feel safe and happy. Although he slept in a hospital bed so I could raise and lower it as needed, I pushed our beds together so we could still sleep beside each other.

The Easy Stand fit perfectly in the living room, so every afternoon, I pulled it out for Brian's standing sessions and then tucked it away when he was done. Our futon couch doubled as his therapy table—it was sturdy and spacious enough for me to lie him down and do his stretches. Each room had a window, and I made curtains and placed plants beneath them, bringing warmth and life into our space. Little by little, the dark cloud over our lives was lifting.

To help with Brian's care, I arranged for a home health aide, and we were lucky to have Kristy as our regular one. She was terrific with Brian, and most importantly, I trusted her—something I couldn't say about many of the other aides we had encountered. Susan also visited us every week, and seeing her always made Brian light up. Her visits were the best therapy, whether we listened to music, watched movies, went shopping, or just talked; those moments were the highlight of our week.

We settled into a routine, with most of the day planned around Brian's sitting time. Mornings started early—I made breakfast so he could take his medications with food. After eating, it was off to the shower. Every morning, we showered together, and I never took for granted how much easier and safer it was to have an accessible shower. It was a simple thing, but it made all the difference in starting our day feeling refreshed. Afterward, I shaved him, brushed his teeth, styled his hair, and laid him back in bed to apply lotion and get him dressed.

For years, I cranked his hospital bed up and down—65 cranks to raise it slightly higher than his wheelchair for transfers, then another 65 cranks to lower it again. Eventually, we got an electric hospital bed, which made a world of difference. Dressing him took patience, especially when it came to his compression socks, which helped with circulation. With the help of rubber gloves and baby powder, I made the process smoother. Getting his pants on required carefully rolling him from side to side, and I dressed his upper body by slipping his arms into his shirt before pulling it down completely once he was seated on the bed.

His clothes needed to fit properly, not only for comfort but also to prevent sores from any fabric bunching up underneath him. But beyond practicality, I always wanted Brian to look nice. He wore the same style of clothes he had before he got sick—button-up shirts, turtlenecks, and dress pants with an elastic waistband that I bought a couple of inches longer so they reached his ankles when he sat. I discreetly tucked his leg bag inside his pant leg so no one would see it or even know it was there. No matter what he wore, he always looked great, especially with that beautiful smile of his.

Once Brian was in his chair, he had about three comfortable hours of sitting time. During that window, I made sure to tilt his chair up and down for minor weight shifts. We had time to go for a walk, run errands, sit outside, or do whatever I had planned for the day. Around lunchtime, I set up the Easy Stand and transferred him into it. He enjoyed standing while eating lunch and watching TV, and I always gave him something to do while he stood.

Brian ate regular food without any issues. He never had trouble chewing or swallowing, which amazed doctors and therapists. They often told me that most people with brain injuries struggled with swallowing or choking, but Brian was different in so many ways. I treated him with respect and wanted him to live as everyday a life as possible. I didn't put much stock in what textbooks said about brain injuries—I focused on what worked for him. While I made sure he had a nutritious diet, I also let him enjoy his favorite foods and treats. Although he could eat finger foods on his own, I usually fed him. We had an unspoken rhythm—he'd watch me scoop food onto the fork and open his mouth just in time, or when he saw a straw coming, he'd instinctively sip. It was simple and natural. We were so in sync that it surprised people. It was almost like we had our own language. His eyes and facial expressions told me everything I needed to know. I believe we were connected on a deeper level—mentally and spiritually.

Some people felt uncomfortable around Brian for extended periods because he couldn't talk. If I wasn't in the room to fill the silence, they wouldn't speak at all. However, I never experienced that problem, and neither did my family or a few close friends. Although I missed his voice, we communicated in our own way. I talked to him about anything and everything, and he responded in his own way. I always believed he understood, even if he couldn't answer the way he once did.

After lunch, when he was done standing, it was time for a nap—though, to be honest, I was the one who needed it. Brian needed time off his backside, so I lay him down for an hour. Since I never slept more than three hours at a time due to getting up at night to turn him, exhaustion was a constant battle. He could stay on his left side for up to three hours, but his left hip caused him terrible pain due to abnormal bone growth in the tissue. Someone once described the pain as feeling like a knife stabbing into the muscle. His right side was more comfortable, and he could stay on it for four hours, but I had to be careful not to overdo it. If he developed a sore on his good side, it would be catastrophic. Some nights, I had to change the sheets, and other nights, Brian simply couldn't sleep, so I stayed up with him. Even on the best nights, I was up at least three times. The physical demands of caregiving left me exhausted, and on top of that, I struggled with anemia. Without health insurance, I suffered for years without knowing the cause. It wasn't until much later that I discovered I had celiac disease. Wheat and grains were damaging my small intestine, making it impossible to absorb nutrients properly. That discovery made my dedication to our diet even more essential for both of us, and I became a master at power napping.

After positioning Brian comfortably for his nap, I put on music or an audiobook for him so I could rest. In the afternoons, I usually had an aide come in so I could go for a run. In the early years, I needed help transferring Brian on and off the futon for therapy, but later, I got a B-Easy transfer board, which allowed me to do it on my own. I never missed a day of his exercises. Under my care, Brian gained weight, got stronger, and his posture improved. Every day, I lay him on his stomach for about 30 minutes—it helped stretch his hip flexors, relieved pressure from his back and tailbone, and even strengthened his neck muscles. We joked that he had a "bionic neck" because he could lift his head endlessly. Many people with his level of disability needed a headrest on their wheelchairs, but he never did. Just by looking at him, it wasn't immediately obvious what his disability was.

Evenings were spent watching TV, listening to music, or reading aloud. It was essential that Brian had fresh air, healthy food, plenty of water, exercise, and mental stimulation every day—otherwise, the monotony would keep him up at night. I tried to add variety to our routine, but those core elements remained the same.

The final transfer of the day—getting him into bed—marked the twelfth transfer on an average day. After undressing him, I ended each night with a foot and leg massage. I had studied reflexology and carefully worked each toe and pressure point. I knew and loved Brian's body better than I knew my own.

***

Although nothing about our lives was normal, one constant remained—our consistently bad experiences with doctors. In France, doctors often made decisions without consulting me and frequently avoided communication altogether. When we moved to the U.S., we found that many doctors were arrogant and indifferent. They treated Brian as if he were less than human and rarely spoke to me directly.

We scheduled appointments weeks in advance to see specialists, only to sit for hours in the waiting room before being called back— just to wait even longer. When the doctor finally arrived, they had often not even glanced at Brian's file. He wasn't there for something routine like a cold or a broken toe—he was a unique patient with complex needs. Yet, there was never any respect or compassion. They scheduled just five minutes for him—five minutes! It was beyond discouraging. Brian deserved better than that. Everyone does, especially considering the outrageous fees they charge. We weren't just names in their medical textbooks to be skimmed over and forgotten the moment they shut the door. I rarely felt anything but disdain for them.

When we first moved to Lincoln, Brian needed a primary care physician to refill prescriptions and authorize home healthcare services. One day, he had an earache. He rubbed his ear, and when I asked if it hurt, he managed to say "ugh huh." My sister and I recorded it. As heartbreaking as it was to see him in pain, we were overjoyed that he had been able to express it. I had also noticed red spots on his feet, so I scheduled an appointment and arranged HandiVan transportation. It was an all-day ordeal. Even with an appointment, we waited for an hour in the crowded waiting room, exposing Brian to germs that could have severe consequences due to his compromised immune system. Complaining never helped, no matter how polite I was—the doctor's office always had an excuse. "She's swamped," they'd say, as if it weren't her own fault for deliberately overbooking every single day. No other profession is as blatantly disrespectful of its clients as the medical field.

When we were finally called back, the nurse took Brian's blood pressure and temperature while I removed his shoes and socks so the doctor could examine the red spots. It was the second time I had brought him in for them. She looked in his ears and saw some wax buildup, deciding to flush them out. Brian, still in his wheelchair, flinched and resisted as she squirted cold water into his ear—who wouldn't? Then, out of nowhere, she casually said, "I spoke with a specialist about the red spots on Brian's feet. If they don't go away, we'll have to amputate."

The words hit me like a freight train. I couldn't breathe. My mind went blank. The room spun. We didn't even finish the ear flush—she just handed me some drops and sent us home. I was in a daze, barely functioning. Tears streamed down my face, and I couldn't stop them.

On the way home, the HandiVan driver asked if I was okay. No, I was not okay. I couldn't believe this was our life. I loved Brian. I loved every part of him, from his hair to his feet. The very idea of cutting them off was unbearable. He had played tennis on those feet. I still held onto hope that he would walk again. And even if he never did, I couldn't fathom amputating them. I would rather die than watch them take his feet.

That night, I spiraled. I couldn't close my eyes without seeing his feet, severed from his body. The thought made me physically ill. What would they do with them? Cremate them? Throw them in the trash? It was too much. For the first time, I thought about ending it all. But I couldn't leave Brian alone in the world. If I went, he would have to go with me—a murder-suicide. The thought horrified me, but I was drowning in despair. I didn't see a way forward.

I ignored my ringing phone all day, but thankfully, I answered later that night. My family was desperate to hear how the appointment had gone, but I couldn't even form words. I was hysterical. My mom, worried for my safety, called Susan. When Susan called, she asked me to repeat exactly what the doctor had said. "Did a specialist actually examine Brian's feet?"

No.

The doctor had only claimed to have spoken with a specialist. No one else had even looked at Brian's feet. Susan snapped me out of my panic. "Brian needs to see a specialist before you start worrying about amputation," she said firmly. "There has to be another option."

She was right. With her help, we made it through that dark time. She called the University of Nebraska Medical Center in Omaha and scheduled an appointment with a vascular surgeon. I had been ready to give up. But Susan saved me that night.

I reached out to the League of Human Dignity; they provided an advocate, and both Kristy and Susan accompanied us to Brian's appointment in Omaha. I needed support—someone to help me ask the right questions and to be there in case the news was bad.

Dr. Baxter entered the crowded exam room and immediately picked up on how deeply Brian was loved and cared for. He was gracious, kind, and gentle—everything the previous doctor had not been. Thank God! It was such a relief to have a positive experience with a doctor, finally. He apologized for the mistreatment and misdiagnosis Brian had endured and reassured me that amputation was nowhere near necessary. There were many options to improve Brian's circulation long before such an extreme measure would even be considered. I could have hugged him.

Dr. Baxter explained that poor circulation is common in people who are wheelchair-bound. Without movement, blood has a harder time returning from the legs to the heart. However, there were solutions—better compression stockings and medication to improve circulation. That was it—a simple fix. A weight lifted off my shoulders, and for the first time in days, I could breathe again. The dark cloud that had consumed me began to clear, but in its place, anger took over. How could that other doctor so casually tell me Brian needed his feet amputated? How could she say something so devastating without even having a specialist examine him? I had nearly lost myself in grief over a misdiagnosis.

With the help of the League of Human Dignity, I wrote a letter to both the doctor and her supervisor, calling out the mishandling, misdiagnosis, and mistreatment of Brian. I wanted accountability—I wanted her to face consequences for her carelessness. When I met with the clinic's director of physicians, he was utterly indifferent. He wasn't even polite. It was clear that to them, Brian was just another Medicaid patient—one among many, insignificant in their eyes. There was money to be made elsewhere, so what did it matter that one patient had been mistreated? I knew then that I wasn't going to waste any more of my time fighting them. I terminated her as Brian's doctor and walked away.

Dr. Baxter prescribed a low-dose blood pressure medication, and that was it. We never had to return to his office or adjust the dosage. His diagnosis and treatment were simple and effective. I'll always be grateful to him. Ironically, the first truly positive doctor experience we had was with someone we only saw once.

***

By the spring of 1992, things were finally starting to look up for us. We had the backyard all to ourselves since the other residents, all wheelchair-bound, never used their back doors. Brian and I often sat on our patio, enjoying the fresh air and quiet moments together. But something was missing. I longed for a dog. I had always loved dogs, having grown up with our family pets—Duffy, Pal, Maggie, and her pups, Pooh and Oreo. Brian loved animals too. We had once dreamed of having both pets and children, but after everything that had happened, I no longer considered having kids. A dog, however, felt right. After so much loss and sadness, I craved something good, something that would bring joy back into our lives.

I had read about the benefits of dogs for people with disabilities, and while I knew those studies were true, the honest reason I wanted a dog was simple—I needed companionship. I wanted a little dog to play with, to love, and to brighten our days.

One warm summer evening, as Brian and I sat on the patio like we had so many times before, I felt it in my heart that I had to get a dog. I called my mom to ask for her opinion, expecting some hesitation, but to my surprise, she was all for it. She excitedly told me about a neighbor's Shih Tzu, a small and adorable breed she was sure I would love. I had never heard of a Shih Tzu before. Our past dogs had been a mix. Duffy was a Poodle, Pal a Labrador, Maggie was a mutt, and so were her pups. Growing up, we had always adopted from the pound, and that was my plan too—to save a dog from a shelter and give it a home. I knew I wanted a small dog, though. After a few bad experiences with large dogs, I was afraid of them.

Just for fun, I flipped through the classified ads in the newspaper—this was long before the internet—and spotted an ad for a litter of Shih Tzus. I called the number and spoke with Lila, the breeder. She had black-and-white purebred puppies, with one male still available. Excited, I told her I wanted to see him. There was a problem, though—she lived in the country, too far for me to bike, and I didn't have a car. Lila mentioned that she would be in town the next morning for a meeting, but if I wanted the puppy, I'd have to take him right away since she couldn't leave him in a hot car all day. I hesitated. I couldn't imagine bringing home a puppy sight unseen. Disappointed, I thanked her and declined. But I couldn't stop thinking about it. For hours, I went back and forth, torn between caution and my growing excitement. Finally, I called my mom again and asked if she was absolutely sure I'd like a Shih Tzu. Without hesitation, she reassured me that I would. That was all I needed to hear. I called Lila back and told her to bring the puppy in the morning. And just like that, it was decided. Life would never be the same again.

It was late in the evening, so I didn't have a chance to buy any supplies for the puppy, but that didn't matter. I was absolutely over the moon with excitement. I hadn't felt this kind of joy since Brian and I got married. I was literally jumping up and down, unable to contain my happiness. Even Brian caught my enthusiasm as I talked nonstop about our new puppy. I had already chosen a name—Zoe. I knew it was traditionally a girl's name, but I didn't care, and I was certain our little dog wouldn't either. The name held deep meaning for me. I wanted to honor my dear friend, Madame Cazemajou. Of course, I couldn't name a puppy after her full name, and I had never called her by her first name, Denise. But she often spoke of her granddaughter, Zoe, with such warmth and love that her face would light up every time she said the name. I wanted that.

I adored my husband with all my heart, but there was an ache inside me—a longing to pour my love into someone the way a mother loves her child. Zoe. Just saying the name filled me with happiness. And now, I, too, would light up when I spoke of *my* Zoe.

I called each of my three sisters with the same high-pitched, squealing excitement, announcing that I was going to be a mama and they were going to be aunts. I was so giddy I couldn't sleep. I kept Brian up all night talking about our new puppy, imagining all the joy he would bring into our lives. For the first time in over a year, our sleepless night wasn't caused by stress or grief—it was pure happiness. Zoe was already changing our lives, and we hadn't even met him yet.

By morning, I was pacing, my eyes glued to the window, waiting for Lila's truck to pull up with our Zoe. It was July 14th, 1992—a day I will remember forever. I couldn't keep still. My heart pounded with anticipation. When she finally arrived, I could hardly wait for her truck to come to a complete stop before I was at her window. And there he was! A tiny ball of black and white fluff nestled on her lap— my Zoe. I let out a squeal and asked to hold him.

"Of course," she said with a smile. "He's yours."

The moment I scooped him up, my heart melted. He was impossibly small, light as air, fitting perfectly in the palm of my hand. And just like that, I loved him. Instantly. Deeply. Completely. From that moment on, my love for him was pure, genuine, and unwavering. He seemed pretty happy with me, too. After I paid Lila and gathered a few dos and don'ts, it was official—I was now responsible for this tiny life. I was a mama. Bursting with excitement, I ran inside to show Brian. He was still in bed, so I gently placed Zoe beside his face. Without hesitation, Zoe started licking him. Brian's entire face lit up as he laughed, his joy so pure it brought tears to my eyes. I guided his hand so he could pet Zoe, and in that moment, it was settled—Brian was his daddy. We were a family.

Chapter Eleven
Running Toward Myself

July 14th wasn't just the day Zoe came to live with us. It became *our* birthday—the day we were given a chance at happiness again, a chance to hope. And all it took was Zoe, just being Zoe. He changed our lives forever.

I asked Kristy to stay with Brian and Zoe while I ran to the store for a few essentials. She was overjoyed for us; she had never seen us this happy before. As both a loyal aide and a dear friend, Kristy had shared in my tears of heartache, helping care for my beautiful husband as illness took its toll. And now, she shared in our tears of joy.

At the store, I picked up everything Zoe would need—a food and water dish, a tiny collar, a leash, a soft bed, and a brush for his fluffy coat. Since he was so little, I opted for a cat harness instead of a regular collar, afraid it might be too much for his delicate frame. Lila had given me some of the food he'd been eating, so I bought the same kind. I didn't want to change a thing until we had seen a vet and knew what was best for him.

From the moment Zoe arrived, he became our entire world. I couldn't put him down. I stroked his soft fur, helped Brian pet him, brushed him, and played with him endlessly. Every hour, I took him outside and celebrated each tiny success—every time he did his business outside, he was met with praise and excitement. He caught on quickly. Since I was home all day with Brian, potty training was easy.

That first night, I made up a cozy little bed for Zoe just outside our bedroom door. To soothe him, I wrapped a wind-up clock in a towel to mimic his mother's heartbeat. I placed the clothes hamper in the doorway so he wouldn't wander into the room. But after settling Brian into bed, I heard the faintest sound from Zoe—not quite a whimper, just a slight noise. Without hesitation, I scooped him up and placed him in bed with us, tucking him gently against my chest. And from that night forward, for the rest of his life, that's where he would sleep. No longer did he need his mother's heartbeat to comfort him—he had mine.

I love getting outside for fresh air every day, so whenever the weather allowed, we went for a walk. Since Brian's disability made it impossible for him to operate an electric wheelchair, I pushed him. We lived near a bike path, and I had seen service dogs walking beside wheelchairs, so I immediately started training Zoe to do the same. At first, I worried that his tiny body might get caught under the wheels, but he was a fast learner. When he got tired, I picked him up, holding him in one arm while pushing Brian with the other. As he grew, I started placing him on the backrest of Brian's wheelchair by his shoulders, where he could comfortably perch while I pushed. Wanting a more secure solution, I brainstormed ways to modify Brian's wheelchair to accommodate Zoe. After some trial and error, I found that hanging a duffle bag over the handlebars on the back worked best. A backpack didn't sit quite right—Zoe would slide to the bottom and couldn't see out. But in the duffle bag, he could stretch out comfortably with his head poking out to watch the world go by. He took to it instantly and loved his new spot, quickly becoming known as "the dog in the bag." With Zoe riding along, we could walk as long as we wanted and take him everywhere.

If we went into a store, I would drape a jacket over the back of Brian's chair, and no one ever noticed Zoe nestled inside. Years later, I found a mesh dog carrier that zipped up and fit perfectly on the back of the wheelchair, making it even easier to bring him along. There was nowhere we couldn't take him; he went grocery shopping, to the zoo, to the movies, and even to doctor appointments. If he made a noise, I'd simply cough or ignore it. Just in case we were ever caught, I had my story ready: Zoe was my service dog, trained to alert me if Brian was about to have a seizure. But no one ever questioned him, and most never even realized he was there.

Zoe was a joy. He happily let me dress him up in sweaters, a bomber jacket, a raincoat, t-shirts, and even pajamas. One year, I had our Christmas cards printed with a picture of him in his Santa outfit. He was always well-groomed, with his signature short haircut and a little ponytail on top. He soaked up every bit of attention and strutted around with pride, as if he knew just how cute he was. I often joked that he sashayed so much he was bound to throw a hip out one day.

Children especially loved spotting him on the back of Brian's wheelchair. More than once, while standing in line at a store, a child at eye level with Zoe's bag would excitedly point and whisper, "Look, there's a dog!" Their mothers, flustered, would shush them and quickly pull them away, scolding them for staring at someone in a wheelchair, never realizing that, indeed, there really was a little dog riding along.

Zoe brought us pure joy. He was playful and full of energy, and Brian loved watching him zoom around our apartment and backyard. When I helped Brian onto the futon for his daily exercises, Zoe would pounce on him, licking his face and ears until Brian was in fits of laughter. When it became too much, Brian would point his finger and say, "Ah, ah, ah," in a mock scolding tone. Their bond was something special. Zoe just knew that Brian needed extra love. He licked him as if he were caring for him, and Brian did his best to pet him, sometimes with my help.

When Zoe rode in the bag on the back of Brian's wheelchair, he took his role as protector seriously. If we passed a big dog, he would bark or growl, standing guard over Brian. At home, he was always alert, barking when someone knocked at the door. But the moment I let them in, he'd greet them happily. Every now and then, if a man walked in, he would take a little longer to warm up, as most of the people in our lives were women. But there was one time when Zoe wasn't so welcoming. A new nurse came for Brian's monthly checkup, filling in for our regular nurse who was out sick. From the moment she walked through the door, Zoe reacted differently. He didn't just bark, he growled, deep and steady, and wouldn't stop. He took refuge under the couch, watching her with suspicion for the entire visit. I wasn't worried that Zoe would hurt her. I was worried because I had never seen him act that way. He clearly sensed something off about her. She tried to dismiss it, saying Zoe must smell her own dog, but plenty of people who visited us had pets, and he had never reacted like that before or since. I trusted Zoe's instincts. I never wanted that nurse back in our home.

Life in Lincoln was improving. With Brian and our little dog, we were a family, and as long as we had each other, we were okay. But Brian's illness brought ongoing challenges, and his neurological damage caused issues with his hip, requiring a bone scan.

For the first time, I had to leave Zoe home alone. Wanting to keep him safe, I set him up in our spacious bathroom, which had a tiled floor—an easy cleanup if he had an accident. I made sure he had everything he might need: his bed, food, water, toys, and treats. Kneeling beside him, I told him I loved him, gave him one last kiss, and closed the door.

The bone scan took six exhausting hours. Brian had to drink a radioactive cocktail and then wait as it slowly spread through his body before the scan could begin. By the time we got home, we were drained. My mind was on getting Brian settled, but I also worried about Zoe, though I reassured myself that he'd be fine for a few hours. I couldn't have been more wrong. The moment I opened the front door, I knew something was terribly wrong. There was no barking, no whining—only silence. My heart pounded as I rushed to the bathroom door. When I opened it, the scene before me was like something out of a nightmare. Zoe lay motionless in a puddle of blood. The walls and floor were smeared with bloody paw prints—evidence of his desperate attempts to escape. He had scratched at the door, then the walls, jumping, clawing, bleeding, until he collapsed from sheer exhaustion. Panicked, I scooped him up and ran outside, desperate for help. By some miracle, our neighbor's mother was visiting, and she immediately offered to drive me to the vet while our neighbor stayed with Brian.

The vet, a kind and gentle woman, sprang into action the moment I burst through the door, cradling Zoe in my arms. She and her assistant worked swiftly, both on him and on calming me down. After a thorough examination, they decided he needed to stay overnight. Tears streamed down my face as I kissed Zoe's tiny head and whispered how sorry I was for leaving him alone. I felt sick with guilt.

Back home, I called Kristy and told her what had happened. She rushed over and helped clean the bloody paw prints from the bathroom. I couldn't bear to look at them—they were a haunting reminder of how much Zoe had suffered in those few short hours. To this day, the memory still haunts me. Zoe's wounds were treated with antibiotics, and the vet gave him a tranquilizer and an IV to rehydrate him. Thankfully, he was strong enough to come home the next day. Our kind vet even washed the blood off him before I arrived, and when I saw him, he looked surprisingly well. His little tail wagging, his eyes bright with relief, he was beyond happy to see me, and I didn't let him out of my arms for days.

For at least a week, his tiny paws barely touched the ground. I held him every chance I could, reassuring both of us that he was safe. The separation anxiety that gripped him now gripped me, too. I was terrified to leave him alone again, just as I feared leaving Brian for more than a few hours. Experience had taught me that in my absence, terrible things could happen to the ones I loved. But I also knew I had to find a way to help Zoe feel secure when we weren't home. Our vet suggested obedience training, and though we attended one free introductory class, I quickly realized that traditional training wasn't what I wanted for Zoe. I wasn't looking for tricks or rigid obedience. He was already an incredible companion, especially with Brian. All I needed was for him to feel calm and safe when left alone.

At our vet's recommendation, I decided to try crate training. She emphasized that the kennel shouldn't feel like a punishment but rather a comfortable, familiar space. I bought a large enough crate for him to stand and turn around in, then lined it with a soft blanket. For several days, I didn't force him inside. Instead, I set it up in the living room near the couch and casually referred to it as his "bed." To make it inviting, I placed treats inside, letting Zoe explore at his own pace. At first, he only poked his head in to grab a treat and quickly backed out. But gradually, he grew more comfortable, eventually sitting inside while I sat beside him on the floor. I never wanted him to associate the kennel with being abandoned—it needed to be a safe place, not a confinement. Over time, the crate became exactly that—a cozy, reassuring spot where he could rest when we were out. It gave him security, and it gave me peace of mind, knowing he had a space of his own.

Running is my form of meditation—I'm not the fastest, but my endurance makes up for it. I tried to go out and run whenever I could, even though my spare time was limited. I attempted to take Zoe along, but he loved sprinting in short, explosive bursts. He'd dart off like a bat out of hell, and I couldn't keep pace. That's when I decided to try rollerblading—a fun, different way to get moving. With the bike path only a few blocks from our apartment, I could glide for miles without worrying about cars. I even gave rollerblading a shot with Zoe, and he absolutely adored it. He was my little muscle dog—joyfully running, as if he were smiling the whole time.

Though I was always reluctant to leave Brian alone, especially during winter, I knew Zoe sometimes needed a quick run to burn off his energy. We'd leave Brian for a few minutes, and as I rollerbladed down the street with Zoe by my side, he'd dash two blocks full throttle, sniff around, and then sprint back home as if eager to see his "daddy." We'd call out, "Let's go see Brian!" and that routine brought us all a bit of lightness for several months.

Then one day, while rolling along together, Zoe suddenly stopped and collapsed, panting heavily. I had to let go of his leash carefully so I wouldn't yank him as I slowed down. I picked him up and carried him home, my heart sinking with worry. The next day, a vet visit confirmed that Zoe had a heart murmur—a leaking valve, likely inherited from his purebred lineage. He would need lifelong heart medication and a diuretic, and rollerblading was off the table. He could still run or walk at his own pace, but I never pushed him too hard. If he ever overdid it, I would carry him in my arms or in his bag. I cried all the way home. With a disabled husband and a disabled dog, I often wondered why we couldn't just be "normal." Our lives were fragile and precious, but somehow, we managed to hold on. In the end, I realized it was a blessing that Zoe had a safe place to be cared for, and as long as I could cuddle him and dote on him, I was happy—we had each other, and that was what mattered most.

When I was a kid, I used to cringe at the way my grandmother cooed over her poodle, and I vowed never to do that with my own dog. But then I met Zoe. One look at his little face, and I couldn't help but talk to him like he was my baby—"Mama loves you!" It felt natural, and soon, it only made sense to call my mom "Granny" when I addressed Zoe. My mom loved the new title, and Zoe adored his Granny. She spoiled him with treats and care during her visits with

Brian and him, even feeding him from her plate, just as she had with our old dog, Maggie. Although I was initially horrified and asked her to stop, it was too late—Zoe quickly learned to wait eagerly for table scraps. I continued to work with Brian on feeding himself. He could reach into a bowl of popcorn or Cheerios and munch while watching TV, though he was a bit messy—just as much food would fall on the floor as made it into his mouth. Zoe would scoop up every dropped morsel and eventually began to beg. I couldn't scold him because I had even encouraged him to help clean up after Brian. Instead, I just laughed at how adorable he was. Later, Zoe even sat on a chair at the table with us; we were a family.

***

In the fall of 1995, I began taking classes at the University of Nebraska-Lincoln, my freshman year at my hometown college, a step I'd always planned on continuing, though now it was five years after Brian's illness. I applied for financial aid and scholarships, and I even posted ads and made calls to find someone to stay with Brian. Since we were only allowed two hours a day of home health aide support, I used that limited time to attend class. Yet, as vital as finishing my education was, running remained my sanctuary. Though all my energy was focused on caring for Brian, I recognized that running was essential for my well-being—something I had to continue even with all the challenges of balancing school and care.

I started running when I was 12 in rural Nebraska, back when it wasn't really a thing. I excelled in gym class and loved sprinting up the hills during our house-building days. I vividly remember seeing a man running in Hidden Valley. It sparked something in me, and soon I was running the Hidden Valley "Circle," a nine-tenths-of-a-mile loop. Before long, that became too small, and I ventured out on the gravel road to town and eventually to the State Park. In high school, I ran cross country—not competitively, but purely for the joy of it. My long, tight hamstrings needed about half a mile to find their rhythm, syncing with the steady beat of my heart and the crunch of gravel beneath my feet. It wasn't just exercise; it was meditation. With every run, the problems that had plagued me would gradually fade away.

As Brian's condition stabilized and I began to live more independently—on my own terms—I realized I had to take care of myself, too. I had to let go of the dreams and hopes we once shared and make new plans. Running, eating healthily, and pursuing my education became my anchors, guiding me to stay true to myself, even in the face of loss and adversity.

Respite care meant that our aide didn't perform hands-on tasks for Brian—they kept him company so he wasn't alone. We were incredibly fortunate to find Doris, who volunteered with Catholic Social Services in her spare time. When she reached out to us, I explained our situation, and we immediately took a liking to her. She was warm, friendly, and talkative, and I felt completely at ease leaving Brian with her from day one; he, too, enjoyed her company. Doris's two grown daughters, Melissa and DeAnn, also volunteered an hour each week, giving me the chance to go for a run. I can't imagine what I'd have done before meeting them. Unlike many others who simply sat and watched TV, unsure of how to interact with Brian, Doris and her daughters engaged with him just like family would. Before long, Brian began to look forward to his respite time—it was good for both of us to have a little time apart.

Throughout my semesters, I enrolled in two classes so I could make full use of the two-hour daily respite care for Brian while still attending my lectures. This schedule even left me time to run errands or go for a run, thanks to the support of Doris, Melissa, and DeAnn. I took one class on Mondays, Wednesdays, and Fridays, and the other on Tuesdays and Thursdays, and even squeezed in a summer school semester to keep my schedule consistent. We lived just two and a half miles from campus, so I rode my bike to class, no matter the weather—rain, shine, sleet, or snow—since the bus never meshed with our timing.

Completing my degree took six long years, but every moment in class was balanced by the time I dedicated to Brian's care—handling his therapy, transfers with the Easy Stand, and every other need, all by myself. While I was away, Zoe would keep watch from the couch. After about an hour and a half, Brian would gaze at the door, and Zoe stood on his back legs with his front paws out for balance like a little prairie dog, stretching his neck to see when I'd return. When I finally opened the door, I was met with instant, joyful chaos. Brian would let out his familiar "ah ah ah," and Zoe's exuberance would erupt in playful jumps and barks. I'd ask, "Did you take good care of Brian?" and reward his efforts with a treat. Those were truly happy years for us.

In the evenings, I would read my schoolwork aloud to Brian and Zoe—a comforting ritual that started long before Brian fell ill. Even when his eyes grew tired from studying music, I'd read to him, and that practice continued through his hospital stay. Sometimes, Zoe would seem a little jealous, nuzzling into my arms or sitting at my desk, pawing at my papers as if to ask why I wasn't paying more attention to him.

Meanwhile, Brian found solace in watching TV and movies. He loved *Jeopardy*—so much so that he'd get upset if I interrupted his viewing, his eyes lighting up as if he already knew the answers. He also adored *The Return of the Pink Panther*, a favorite from before his illness that he never lost. His ongoing passion for tennis, especially when listening to John McEnroe's commentaries, reassured me that deep down, he was still the same vibrant Brian. In those quiet evenings, our little routine, a mix of reading, shared glances, and familiar screen scenes, became a beacon of normalcy and connection. I was happy.

For six years, Doris, Melissa, and DeAnn became like family. Every Christmas Eve, they'd visit to exchange gifts and sing carols. I'll never forget that one ice storm when we lost power for three days—Doris came by with hot soup and checked on us. Their weekly support, though it may have seemed small, was invaluable. It was one hour a week for six years! But it was so much more than that; it gave me a break from my responsibilities and helped me achieve so many of my dreams. Because of their support, I was able to attend UNL and earn my Bachelor of Arts degree, and even run two marathons, a lifelong dream of mine. In the spring of 2000, when a neighbor casually asked if I was training for a race, something inside me stirred. I'd always said, "One day, I'll run a marathon." That day, I decided, why not now? Fueled by inspiration from school and the gentle push of hope, I threw myself into a challenging sixteen-week training program.

With Doris, DeAnn, Melissa, and my sister Susan by my side, I trained hard and ran the Omaha Marathon on August 26, 2000. The exhilaration of chasing that dream filled me with pure joy—a joy that radiated to both Brian and Zoe. On marathon day, my mom stayed with Brian while I set off, secure in the care provided by a trusted home health aide. I woke early, got Brian dressed so the aide had to do minimal assistance, and Melissa drove me to Omaha—she even ran the half-marathon herself. Our families came together to cheer me on. The race was grueling—humidity, heat, and tough hills made my legs cramp and forced me to walk part of the course. Just when I felt ready to give up, Melissa appeared beside me and ran silently with me. Her presence, along with that of my sisters, gave me the strength to carry on in the marathon and in real life. Georgia flew in from Wisconsin, and Liz joined from Rhode Island, with Susan and my dad by my side. I choked back tears and crossed that finish line, overwhelmed by a sense of accomplishment. That day will always be a reminder that no matter the challenges, I had the support to chase my dreams and create a life filled with hope. For me, it was the love and support of my family that carried me through to the finish line.

I felt the momentum of life. I excelled in school and pledged to keep running. I ran the Lincoln marathon the following May. It wasn't as exhilarating as my first marathon, but it brought me a feeling of achievement and hope. I will forever be grateful for the love and support Doris, Melissa, and DeAnn gave me throughout the years. No matter how difficult our circumstance were, I felt God/the Universe brought people into my life to help me through it: Madame Cazemajou, Jill and Peter, Cindy and Mark, Gail and Loren, Linda and Olivier, Jeff and Diana, Jeff and Camille, Doris, Melissa, DeAnn, Mary, Marleen, my mom, my dad, Susan, Georgia, Liz, Kristy, Brian and Zoe. I could not have done it without their love and support.

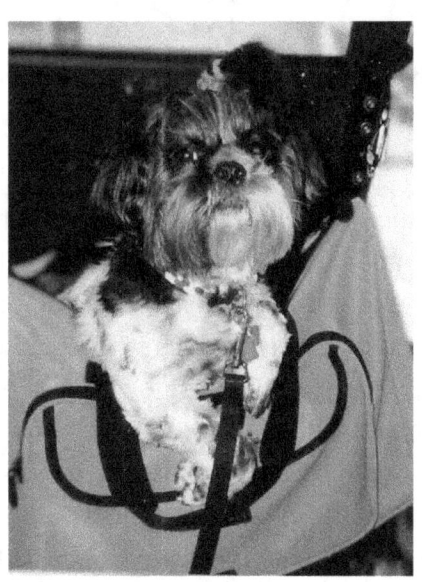

Chapter Twelve
Freedom on Four Wheels

In the spring of 1997, Brian's alma mater, Valley City State College in North Dakota, was hosting their annual EBC Hit Parade. His music fraternity wanted to pay tribute to him—his old friends, long before I knew him, had come together to do something special after hearing about his illness. They even rented a minivan to drive us up, and I arranged for us to stay with some friends I had met while Brian was in the hospital in Fargo. My mom joined us for support. Their kindness touched me, though I knew the day would be both emotional and challenging.

Traveling with Brian was never easy. Even with the rented minivan, his condition made long rides difficult, and we had to pack countless supplies and equipment. Simple tasks like showering and using the bathroom became complicated, and without our hospital bed and Easy Stand—too big to bring along—Brian couldn't stand during our trips. I worried constantly about germs and infections when performing his catheterization outside our home, where I had to use a strict sterile technique. There were so many factors to consider, but I did it all for Brian. I wanted him to know he wasn't forgotten; I wanted him to feel the care of all those whose lives he had touched.

Our journey from Lincoln to Fargo was usually an eight-hour drive in good conditions. However, after reaching Sioux Falls, South Dakota, we encountered unexpected snow. The roads grew dangerously slippery, and we passed one accident after another. Despite driving cautiously, I hit a patch of black ice just as a semi-truck passed, which sent our minivan careening off the road and into a guardrail. We hit hard and bounced toward oncoming traffic before the van finally stopped just inches from the highway. Brian and I were securely belted in the front, but my mom, seated in the back, was struck by Brian's untethered wheelchair. Zoe, who was also in the back with her, was unharmed, but the experience was terrifying. I screamed for what felt like hours, knowing I was responsible for everyone on board. Thankfully, aside from a few bruises on my mom, we were all physically okay.

A police officer soon arrived and helped us arrange assistance. The minivan was totaled, and we then faced the challenge of transporting Brian and his large, non-folding wheelchair. After some frantic searching, we finally found someone with a truck. I carefully transferred Brian from the minivan to his wheelchair, then into the truck, securing his wheelchair in the back before driving to the nearest hotel.

That day was a stark reminder of how fragile our lives were, yet also of the immense care and love that carried us through every ordeal. Once we were settled in the motel room, I immediately made a flurry of phone calls, first to Susan, then to our EBC friends, to update them on what had happened. At that moment, all I wanted was to go home. We were exactly halfway between Fargo and Lincoln, and although the accident felt like a bad omen, my mom and the spirit of the EBC Hit Parade convinced me to keep going for Brian's sake. They arranged for Daryl and Brian's dad to pick us up in a van, promising to take care of the rest, and I had no choice but to agree.

Brian's dad and Daryl arrived around 2 a.m. We tried to rest, but sleep eluded us. Daryl, so kind and patient, helped me transfer Brian into the luxury van belonging to an EBC family. He drove us to my friend Camille and Jeff's house in Fargo. Camille was a friend I made when I worked at the hospital daycare. By the time we arrived, the sun was just beginning to rise. Brian, exhausted, fell asleep as soon as I got him settled, while I stayed awake, too excited to sleep, eagerly updating my family on our safe arrival.

When Brian and I met, we lived in the same town as my family, so naturally, they got to know him well, while I hardly ever interacted with his family. I only met his relatives briefly at Christmas and our wedding, which wasn't much of a foundation. As the oldest of four, there were significant age gaps—he was eight years older than his brother and twelve years older than his sister, and their bonds had grown somewhat distant when he left for college at 18. I never really forged a deep connection with any of them. When Brian fell ill, our relationship with his family became even more strained—being so far apart both physically and emotionally made communication nearly impossible. Their minimal involvement in Brian's rehabilitation and everyday life left me feeling both puzzled and heartbroken—it seemed as if their absence and lack of inquiry meant they simply didn't care. Even though our relationship was strained, I made an effort to maintain communication by sending letters and making sporadic phone calls to update them on Brian's well-being.

While we were living in Lincoln, Brian's parents and sisters visited a few times, and I always found those encounters awkward. With Brian unable to speak, I ended up carrying the conversation, and when I was doing his stretches, his dad was so uncomfortable that he would sit outside in the car. Once, when his two sisters visited together, our differing perspectives made it hard to connect, and I could sense a deep-seated dislike toward me. I know they loved their brother, but they just couldn't express it. To this day, I remain uncertain about their true feelings because we never had a candid conversation about it. Their lack of involvement in Brian's rehabilitation and daily life was a constant source of anxiety for me— I longed for him to receive the whole love and support of his family. I couldn't understand how those who cared for Brian could choose not to be a part of his recovery, nor could I grasp their apparent animosity toward me despite my unwavering dedication to his care. Letting go of those unanswered questions and lingering emotions has been incredibly difficult. Perhaps my own extraordinary family set my expectations too high, but regardless, Brian's family never truly became a part of our lives. Returning to Fargo and facing his family was stressful, but I kept an open mind, hoping that over time, they would start to open up.

That night, the EBC Hit Parade in Valley City—an hour's drive from Fargo—was a poignant tribute to Brian. I made sure to get him ready so he'd look his best when meeting so many old friends. We arrived a bit late, but they waited until Brian was there before starting the tribute. Surrounded by his family—my cousin Ted, his wife Athena, and their kids—and a full auditorium of well-wishers, the curtain went up and tears flowed. Brian's old friends spoke movingly about the love they had for him, the fun they shared, and their prayers for his recovery. They dedicated the music they once played together to him. It was breathtaking. I sat beside Brian, holding his hand, grateful that he could feel the love around him—a tribute that was far more healing than any funeral could be.

Afterward, everyone stopped to give us hugs and kisses. I still remember happily wiping lipstick off his cheek amid that outpouring of affection. We posed for pictures, though looking at those photos later always brought back the bittersweet memory of our pale, puffy-eyed faces—a reminder of the heartache we endured. It was painful to see Brian, so debilitated in his wheelchair, instead of standing tall beside his old buddies with the vibrancy he once had.

Daryl then helped transfer Brian back into the van to return to our friends' house. As we struggled to get him and his chair into the van, Brian's own family stood there watching. Daryl muttered, "What the hell is wrong with his family?" and strangers nearby asked about them. I had no explanation—Brian's family still baffled me. That's when I realized Daryl had never even met Brian before that night; he belonged to the music fraternity long after Brian had left. Daryl's generosity and kindness deeply moved me—truly, it seemed that strangers cared more about Brian than his own family. And that was something I had heard before, yet it still struck me deeply.

The next day, my friends hosted a lunch for Brian's family and my cousins. When it was time to position Brian for his stretching exercises, his brother—Jon, who had rarely reached out—came to speak with me. He admitted he hadn't been a part of Brian's life and expressed genuine regret. I set aside my hurt to listen, gently reminding him that it was Brian who needed to hear those words. I then offered him the chance to observe our routine. Curious to learn how he might help, he stayed as I demonstrated how simple touches—rubbing Brian's back, massaging his feet, or even just talking—could make a difference. I knew Brian cherished his brother; he had once taught his little brother how to play baseball, and I could see the resemblance between them.

We remained with our friends for another day so Daryl could arrange time off to drive us back home, with Brian's brother joining us. My mom, though bruised and emotionally drained from the accident, kept her spirits up and mingled with Brian's old friends and family. We were all utterly exhausted; emotionally more so than physically, and the long drive home only deepened my gratitude for Daryl's help. I cried throughout the weekend; my eyes were swollen from grief and frustration over how far our lives had shifted. Our daily existence no longer included the warm, loving interactions Brian once enjoyed; most days, only I spoke to him, while others completely ignored him. Despite it all, I found purpose in caring for Brian, loving him, and holding on to hope for both of us. That night, as his brother spent time with us before returning to Fargo, he showed absolute determination to learn how to help. We spoke long into the evening, and I noticed all the physical similarities between him and Brian—reminders of a past that now felt so bittersweet. When we hugged goodbye, there were promises of visits, letters, and phone calls. I hoped that, over time, Jon's presence might help Brian feel less alone.

Afterward, Jon sent a few messages, including an audio recording of a radio broadcast he'd done, which I played for Brian countless times. But a few months later, I injured my back so severely that I couldn't even get out of bed, let alone transfer Brian. Desperate, I asked Susan to help for a few days. She sacrificed time from school and work. Realizing I couldn't rely on her indefinitely, I reached out to Jon again, asking if he could step in while I recovered. He promised to talk to his boss and call back, but he never did. In the meantime, I consulted our home health agency, and a nurse recommended we get a Hoyer Lift for Brian.

In the end, I found a way to manage his care on my own. The last I heard from Jon was a brief call years later to announce he had a baby, and after which I never spoke to him again.

***

In 1992, after losing our family home, my parents relocated to a small town in the Nebraska panhandle. They renovated a house that had once been divided to house railroaders when the coal train stopped running through Chadron. We first visited at Christmas that year, and thereafter, we spent every summer there—except the summer I was training for a marathon. I took summer school, which ended mid-July, just as Lincoln's heat and humidity became unbearable, and then my dad would drive us out. We loaded a trailer with Brian's Easy Stand, his shower chair, wheelchair, wedge, and other essential supplies. Neighbors and HandiVan drivers often stopped by to ask if we were moving, but in reality, we were just gathering everything we needed to survive. My dad even installed a roll-in shower in the downstairs bathroom so we could comfortably stay for several weeks each summer—a welcome escape from the confines of our small apartment in Lincoln.

While we were at my parents' house, I didn't have a home health aide. Instead, my mom stayed with Brian and Zoe in the evenings while I went for runs. During the day, we relaxed in their spacious yard, doing some light yard work, renting movies, and reading. Those few weeks away were a vital respite from our daily routine, and both Brian and Zoe needed that change as much as I did. Brian especially adored spending time with my mom. The love in his eyes whenever she was around was unmistakable. She showered him with attention and affection, and it was clear that both he and Zoe were deeply loved.

Before Brian fell ill, my dad and Brian hardly had a chance to bond. My dad was one of the few men Brian knew after he got sick. Yet my dad always showed his love through acts of service. He built the boardwalk for our wedding, drove hundreds of miles every summer to bring us home, constructed bookshelves and a patio for us, and renovated their home—knocking out walls, installing a roll-in shower, and adding a ramp at the entrance. His tireless work, time, and money made our lives easier, and his acts of love touched me deeply.

My sisters, Georgia and Liz, were always a constant support. Georgia barely knew Brian before our wedding, yet she was always kind and caring toward him, playing a vital role in finding our apartments and rescuing us from that dreadful situation in Kansas. Liz, who had grown closer to Brian in the year before we married, as he was even the only one patient enough to help her get her driver's license, always stayed in touch despite moving around a lot, joining the Coast Guard, and traveling the world. We cherished her letters, phone calls, and visits.

My mom and Brian met even before I did. There's a snapshot from a party just days before I met him that still makes me smile. My mom, like everyone else, was captivated by Brian's natural sparkle. Over the year leading up to our wedding, they grew close, and my mom never would have allowed me to marry him unless she truly loved and respected him, and she did, wholeheartedly. I'm biased, of course, but Brian loved her dearly. I remember how he would race to answer the phone whenever she called while we were in Bordeaux, the conversation shared through an earpiece that allowed him to listen in. After Brian became ill, my mom's care for him deepened into something almost maternal. In her uniquely soothing voice, she reassured him that everything would be all right, showering him with hugs, kisses, and unwavering love by bringing him his favorite foods, buying him nice clothes, and being there when it mattered most. She stood by him through our darkest days and our brightest moments, supporting us in every way possible. I know Brian loved her deeply and would have expressed his gratitude if he could, but I'm sure she knew it all along. His attempts to show her his affection, however subtle, were evident in the way his eyes lit up when she was near.

Then there's Susan. I've often spoken about the special bond she shared with Brian—they loved music, tennis, and movies, and their friendship truly lit up our lives. Susan genuinely respected Brian's opinions, whether about school or music, and he cared for her deeply in return. Even when we were in Bordeaux, Brian eagerly awaited her letters and phone calls, and he was heartbroken to miss her graduation. Their connection grew even stronger after he fell ill; every time she visited, his eyes would light up with a silent, powerful love. Reflecting on all that Susan has done for us still brings tears to my eyes. Beyond being a constant support for me, she was the one who stepped in physically to make our lives as comfortable as possible. She helped with Brian's transfers and stretches, ran countless errands, and drove countless miles— from Omaha to Fargo, Lincoln, or Gering—just to see us. She sacrificed her vacation time, even buying treats on her modest income, reminding me to find moments of joy despite our frugality.

Susan wasn't just there in a practical sense; she filled our days with love and warmth. She spent every holiday with us, even offering her own apartment as a temporary home, and she willingly slept in the living room and gave us the bedroom. After Brian fell ill, she became his most steadfast friend. She treated him with respect, never speaking down to him, and kept him connected to the things he loved—music, tennis, and the everyday conversations they used to share. The love and care she gave went far beyond any familial obligation. Susan would do anything to make Brian smile—even if it meant making a complete fool of herself. For someone usually so modest and quiet, her devotion knew no bounds. And for me, she was a constant pillar of strength, supporting me even when I struggled to feel worthy. I know I've never been half the sister she's been to me, yet she continues to love and support me unconditionally.

Little Zoe became the heartbeat of our family; the purest, fuzziest kind of love. Just by being himself, he filled our days with joy. He was irresistibly cute, our constant source of entertainment, and our pride and joy. Brian's face would light up watching him scamper around the house and yard, and I treasured those moments when we all snuggled together on the couch. Zoe even made Brian's exercises more fun by pouncing on him, licking his face, and making him laugh, distracting him from the intensity of his workout. He served as Brian's little seat warmer, staying in his chair until Brian was ready to transfer back.

In every sense, Zoe helped us become a family. He revived the playful, happy side of me that might otherwise have faded, bringing laughter and love into our lives in ways nothing else could. I can't overstate the profound change his presence brought. He adored Brian, vigilantly protecting him when I wasn't around and keeping a watchful eye over him. Their bond was so deep that it needed no words; their love spoke for itself.

Brian's illness gave us a unique opportunity to express love in ways most people never experience. Loving Brian was a gift, as natural as breathing. In loving him, I discovered the very best in myself. Loving him made life worth living.

***

We lived in Lincoln for nine years, in a modest apartment on the corner of Vine and 44th Street. School became my saving grace as it gave me purpose and much-needed stimulation. I thoroughly enjoyed my classes, the research, and the writing they required. I continued to take two courses each semester, plus a summer session, before spending a few weeks at my parents' house at the end of summer. Meanwhile, Brian began to slow down noticeably. He started taking afternoon naps—something entirely out of character for him. When I raised my concerns with his doctors, they barely took notice. His primary care physician, an internist who seemed more interested in filling prescriptions than in his well-being, simply brushed it off by saying that Brian was "just getting older." I sensed that something was wrong, but I didn't have any answers.

Brian was generally healthy and rarely fell ill—except for one persistent issue: chronic bladder infections. Due to neurological damage, his bladder was under constant strain, causing spasms and incomplete emptying, which made infections almost inevitable. He took medication to help control these contractions, and I would catheterize him three times a day. At the same time, he also took high doses of Vitamin C to keep his urine acidic and discourage bacterial growth. Despite these measures, the bladder infections remained a constant challenge, and we ended up visiting our urologist more often than any other doctor.

In the summer of 2001, we made our annual trip across the state to visit my parents. My dad, retired as a railroad engineer, had always been a pillar for us, but the drive to and from his home was becoming increasingly challenging. While we were there, I made some calls to search for wheelchair-accessible housing nearby. To my delight, I discovered a brand-new three-bedroom home that was fully accessible. I hadn't planned on living in rural Nebraska. Still, the opportunity to live in a spacious house—with room for a garden, enough space to avoid tripping over Brian's equipment, and a yard for Zoe to play in—while staying close to my parents was simply too good to pass up.

At the end of October, we moved into our new home. Susan, along with our friends Diana and Jeff, helped pack up our apartment in Lincoln so that Brian wouldn't have to face the long trip again. My parents helped us move in. That first night was a whirlwind—I had to set up Brian's bed, arrange all his equipment, and unpack his supplies so I could care for him properly. By then, I had become completely independent and no longer relied on a home health agency.

I had big dreams for life in our new home. I even envisioned becoming a foster parent, a substitute teacher, and exploring many other avenues for personal growth. I was grateful to be close to my parents; I kept telling myself it was for their sake as they grew older, though deep down I knew something was wrong with Brian, and I couldn't face it alone. I wrapped up my last two classes at the local college and graduated in December with my Bachelor of Arts degree from UNL. Although I wasn't able to attend the ceremony, receiving that diploma filled me with immense pride. It was a long, challenging journey, but every step was worth it.

I struggled to find dependable respite care—there were few established resources for families like mine. In Lincoln, I already felt the judgmental stares, but in rural Nebraska, it was twice as bad. I even volunteered as a GED tutor, yet the only person I found to help stay with Brian was unreliable. I couldn't commit to anything unless I could bring Brian along, which was deeply discouraging. So, I filled our days reading books aloud to Brian and cherishing the time we spent with my parents.

We soon realized that having our own van was essential. The HandiVan, like we used in Lincoln, wasn't suitable—it was designed mainly for elderly patients heading to hospital appointments and often took over an hour to get us where we needed to go. Living in a remote area—literally at the end of town—only made the situation worse. The nearest grocery store was over a mile away—a distance that, in the harsh wind and bad weather, was simply too challenging to risk exposing Brian to. Social opportunities were scarce in that isolated area, and after I graduated, there wasn't even a nearby school to keep me occupied. When we moved in, I was so excited that I baked cookies and introduced myself to several neighbors, hoping to build friendly relationships. However, it soon became clear that while they were curious, they were far from warm or welcoming. Early on, I realized that moving there was a huge mistake—it was too remote and isolating. Although I appreciated the spacious house and being close to my parents, everything else felt profoundly wrong.

In our first spring there, Social Services forced us to cash out Brian's retirement fund. Although it wasn't much to begin with, his modest teaching salary had gradually accrued enough interest to trigger Medicaid regulations. They insisted that I use the funds—cash them out and purchase Brian's funeral plans within two weeks—otherwise they'd deny him his medical and food benefits. I tried to explain that we couldn't afford to spend that money; it was only a few thousand dollars that we weren't meant to touch until he turned 60, or else we'd lose half of it. They didn't care. Unfortunately, we lost half the money; however, it was just enough to cover Brian's cremation and make a down payment on a van. We eventually found a full-size van that we modified ourselves. While there was assistance available to adapt a van for wheelchair access, no funding was provided to purchase one. We had the roof raised, installed a wheelchair lift, and added retractable tie-downs. That van gave us true freedom. I still remember the joy I felt the first time I drove it. I could take Brian anywhere without ever having to wait for the HandiVan again. We could go grocery shopping whenever we pleased, visit my parents' house, and simply explore. It was life-changing, expensive, but completely worth it.

Chapter Thirteen
Letting Go, Holding On...

W e took a few memorable trips in our van, but one of the most special was on our anniversary—September 2, 2002. Fourteen years after our first date and thirteen years of marriage, we decided to return to Chadron. It was only a two-hour drive each way, but for Brian, it was a big endeavor. He needed regular breaks to relieve the pressure on his body, and while the back seat of the van was converted into a full-size mattress, transferring him inside was a challenge. My mom joined us for support.

Traveling was always an adventure. Brian sat behind me in the middle of the van, and I adjusted the rearview mirror so we could watch each other. I played our favorite music and sang along, stealing glances at him as he smiled that sweet, sexy smile of his. As we neared Chadron, memories flooded back. The old highway leading into town was the same, winding past rolling hills and buttes on the edge of the Pine Ridge Forest. The air carried the scent of pine, sage, alfalfa, and dust—home. Smells have a way of unlocking memories, and in an instant, thirteen years vanished.

Our first stop was downtown. With just one stoplight, Chadron was a town where time seemed to stand still. I worried that things would have changed too much, that my memories wouldn't match reality, but nothing had really changed. We drove through old neighborhoods, past the homes of friends we once knew. Then we stopped at Wilson Park near "our tree," the one where Brian had carved our initials. It felt like the perfect place to sit while Brian rested in the van.

The warmth of the day reminded me of our wedding, though it wasn't quite as windy. Being Labor Day weekend, the park was quiet, almost deserted. And then, at exactly 2 p.m.—the time we had been married thirteen years earlier—a familiar face appeared. Peter, our wedding photographer, happened to walk by. I couldn't believe my eyes. I called out to him, and his expression mirrored my own shock. When we greeted each other, I told him it had been exactly thirteen years to the hour since we last saw him, when he was capturing our wedding day. He smiled and told us that our wedding photo was still the first in his album, the one he showed prospective clients—his very first professional photograph. I don't believe that was just a coincidence. Moments like that feel like whispers from God, reassuring me that life is unfolding as it should.

After Brian's nap, we visited the music hall at the college, where we had met and where Brian once taught. The doors were unlocked, and we had the place to ourselves. We knew that building well; in the year he taught there, we had practically lived in it. I took pictures in the hallway where we first met and outside his old office door. But when I snapped a photo of Brian, a wave of sorrow hit me. The man who had once been so vibrant, so full of talent and life, was now silent and still. How had we come to this? How long has time taken us here?

We sat on the steps, just as we once had, talking about our dreams for the future. Life had certainly not turned out the way we planned. I could see the weight of the day in Brian's eyes, and I knew neither of us could bear to visit our old house on the hill. It would have been too much. So, we climbed back into our van and drove out of town. Just as quickly as time had slipped away when we arrived, so too did the past fade as we left.

Heading back to our home in Gering, I felt grateful for the visit. In a way, it confirmed that everything we had lived was real—not just some beautiful dream I had imagined.

We spent five years in our home on 3rd Street, and I tried to make the most of our time there. I planted a vegetable garden in the backyard, added flowers around the trees in the front, and filled the house with plants. Zoe would sit beside Brian, watching me putter around the yard. He loved feeling the wind on his face, letting it ruffle his fur as he caught the scents in the air. Sometimes, he sat outside, enjoying the day with us. Though he no longer played in the hose and sprinkler as he had when he was younger, he still found joy in being outdoors.

The house gave us plenty of space for all of Brian's equipment. We finally had room for a real dining table, and we could comfortably host family and friends. Zoe loved the house, too. He would race up and down the hallway, darting in and out of the three bedrooms, and happily marking the trees in the yard as his own.

At first, the move had brought new energy into our lives, but over time, the years began to catch up with us. Brian was slowing down significantly. Zoe, too, was sleeping more and struggling to jump onto the bed or couch. I had to start lifting him. Every evening, when I stretched Brian out on the couch, Zoe would wait patiently until I picked him up so he could shower his daddy with kisses. As soon as he was done, he'd leap over to Brian's chair, the most comfortable seat in the house, where he'd curl up and settle in, content as ever.

For a couple of years before our move to western Nebraska, I knew something wasn't right with Brian. The signs were there—he was sleeping more, losing weight, and at times, he didn't seem like himself. Most days, when I looked into his eyes, I saw my Brian, the man I knew and loved. But increasingly, there were moments when it felt like he wasn't there. I even took him to a neurologist, despite my deep skepticism after a terrible experience in Lincoln, where a doctor once told me Brian was having seizures simply because he was laughing. That experience had shattered my trust in the field, but I was desperate for answers. The new neurologist conducted an extensive study of Brian's brain and referred us to a neurosurgeon. Together, they examined the damage and suggested implanting a shunt.

A shunt is a small catheter placed in the brain to drain excess spinal fluid into the abdomen. The doctors explained that because of Brian's brain damage, his brain had shrunk, leaving extra fluid that could be causing problems. But the procedure was risky—any brain surgery carries the potential for permanent damage, and there was no guarantee that draining the fluid would improve Brian's condition. Worse, there was no way to regulate the shunt. If it drained too much fluid, Brian could suffer from chronic infections and severe migraines.

It didn't feel right. I couldn't justify such a dangerous procedure without any certainty that it would help him. Deep down, I also felt that this wasn't really the root of the problem. I didn't know what was wrong, but something in me knew we were nearing the end.

I started letting go of things I had clung to for years. I unpacked a suitcase full of Brian's old clothes, the ones he wore before he got sick. Each tie, every outfit, held memories: where we had gone, what we had done, every small detail frozen in time. I had held onto his shoes for years, the same ones he wore when I first met him. They were so worn that there was a hole in the sole, yet I couldn't bring myself to part with them. It felt like giving up. I wanted to believe that one day, Brian would wear them again. The man who once walked, played tennis, sang, danced, and swept me off my feet. But instinct told me it was time. I took pictures—not that I needed to. Those memories are etched in my mind forever. I couldn't bear to give his clothes to anyone else. They belonged to Brian, and only Brian.

Then there was his music. A large box filled with sheet music, reminders of the musician he once was. I could never give away or sell his saxophone—that was sacred—but I knew I had to do something with the music. I couldn't keep carrying around pieces of the past forever. So, with a heavy heart, I decided to donate his collection to his alma mater, the University of Northern Colorado. But I kept one piece—the last one he had been working on. It still rests in his saxophone case, a quiet reminder of the man he was and the music that lived within him.

Over the years, we managed to take a few more trips—just simple, one-day adventures. I wanted Brian to visit his alma mater, the University of Northern Colorado, one last time, as well as the town of Boulder. Traveling was becoming increasingly complex, though. Brian slept a lot, needed to be catheterized multiple times a day, and without the Easy Stand, he couldn't stretch his legs properly, which made him uncomfortable.

At UNC, we visited Frazier Hall, the music building where Brian had spent countless hours creating and practicing. It was a place filled with memories, not just for him but for me as well—I had spent a summer there with him, and it was deeply sentimental. Boulder, too, held a special place in our hearts. It was the town where we had fallen in love, where we once dreamed of living—a place that embraced the arts and the kind of life we had envisioned for ourselves. But reality had other plans, and we could never afford to make that dream a reality. Walking along the pedestrian shopping mall, I was overwhelmed by memories of happier times. These trips—what felt like "one last time" journeys—were my way of giving Brian a chance to say goodbye to the places he loved, to have some closure.

As Brian's health declined, so did Zoe's. My sweet little companion started making regular trips to the vet. He had been on heart murmur medication, and then a bump appeared on his back leg. It kept growing, and when the biopsy results came back, the news was devastating—it was malignant. The vet recommended surgery, but it wasn't without risk. Because of Zoe's age and heart condition, anesthesia could be dangerous. But if we didn't go through with it, the cancer would take him. The decision was agonizing. I cried endlessly…why was life so unfair? After everything we had already been through, why did my precious Zoe have to suffer too? I wasn't ready to say goodbye to him. He was my source of comfort, my constant, my joy.

The morning of his surgery, I could barely see through my swollen eyes as I dropped him off. The wait felt unbearable, but finally, after several hours, the vet called. The surgery had gone well, and Zoe was ready to go home. Given his severe separation anxiety, the vet agreed that he would recover better at home than at the clinic.

I wasn't sure what to expect when I arrived to pick him up, but I certainly didn't expect to see him standing there with his leash on, ready to leave. He was happy to see me, but his expression said it all— *Get me the hell out of here!* From that moment on, I carried him everywhere and never let him out of my sight. I watched over him carefully, making sure he didn't lick his wound or do anything that could slow his healing. He had been through so much, and I just wanted to protect him.

***

I felt deeply for Christopher Reeve and his wife when he had the accident that left him paralyzed. I followed his journey closely, read his book, and often wondered how different his experience was from ours. With access to the best medical care and top specialists, he didn't have to endure many of the hardships we faced. Yet, despite having the best of everything, he was still a quadriplegic. No amount of fan mail, attention, or well-wishes could change the fact that his life, and the lives of his wife, children, and friends, had been turned upside down.

He openly acknowledged that he received far better care and support than the average person with a spinal cord injury. He also used his platform to bring attention to important issues, such as the young people placed in nursing homes simply because they required extensive care, and the fact that life doesn't have to end after a tragedy.

Still, I often wondered how different our lives would have been if we hadn't had to fight for everything. What if Brian had access to the best doctors, the best caregivers, the best resources? But after reading Christopher's book, I had a realization. Brian *did* have the best of the best. He had *me*. It took me years to fully understand this, but I know now that I was the absolute best advocate and caregiver for him, regardless of money, status, or resources. I was meticulous. Under my care, Brian never developed pressure sores, and he never suffered a fall.

I was shocked to learn about some of the falls and complications Christopher endured, even with around-the-clock professional care. Concerned, I wrote him a letter, hoping to spare him some of the trial and error so many of us had already been through. It made me wonder—why wasn't there a better system in place, a more coordinated program or network of information, for people whose lives are suddenly changed in an instant? The little things I had learned along the way made a world of difference. I also realized how much creativity played a role in caregiving. I was always finding ways to make things easier, more efficient—not just for Brian, but in general. I lacked the engineering skills to turn all my ideas into reality, but I knew there were innovative solutions out there. Unfortunately, most of them were far too expensive for the average person.

One of the biggest challenges in caregiving is preventing falls during transfers. I never understood why Christopher's caregivers didn't use a Hoyer lift. When I injured my back and physically couldn't lift Brian, we got one. It's essentially an engine lift—just marketed for medical use and priced accordingly. Some models even have ceiling tracks installed throughout the home, allowing a person to be moved from room to room without relying on bulky equipment. The lift I ordered was the most practical one available. It came with a vest-like U-sling that was quick and easy to put on. The standard full-sheet sling, which is placed under a person's body, was completely impractical—it was difficult to slide under someone already seated in a chair, uncomfortable to sit on all day, and useless for transfers to the toilet or shower chair. The U-sling, on the other hand, wrapped around Brian's torso, with two wide straps that crisscrossed between his legs, leaving his lower body free for easier transfers. I preferred doing a pivot transfer without the Hoyer whenever possible, but I kept it—just in case I ever needed it again.

There were small but significant things that made caring for Brian much easier. A pull sheet across his bed allowed me to turn him from side to side without pulling on his body. Bed rails provided extra security, preventing any risk of him falling out of bed. The roll-in shower eliminated the dangers associated with bathroom transfers, making bathing significantly safer.

I found creative solutions for everyday challenges—such as using baby powder and rubber gloves to make it easier to slide on compression stockings. For medication, I crafted a simple mouth prop from popsicle sticks to help me place pills at the back of his throat. Crushing and mixing them into food would have ruined his appetite, so this method ensured he could take them without discomfort.

Today, there are even more innovative products designed to improve the quality of life. Advanced urinary care solutions offer greater convenience and dignity. Adaptive clothing—such as backless jackets, Velcro closures, elastic waistbands, longer inseams, and friction-free bottoms—makes dressing easier and more comfortable for individuals with mobility challenges. These small adaptations can make a world of difference in daily care and overall well-being.

Christopher Reeve sent a response to my letter. Knowing he had received it meant a lot to me. Maybe, in some small way, it made a difference in his life—I hope so. He and Dana shared a special bond, and I would have loved the chance to meet them, but sadly, I never did. I followed his journey closely, watching his progress with therapy and his advocacy for stem cell research. We were fortunate that he chose to go public about his life after the accident. He brought awareness, hope, and a sense of possibility to so many around the world.

Like Christopher, I believe in the potential for recovery—or at the very least, improvement. It frustrates me when people are told they will never walk again or when therapy is denied simply because progress isn't deemed significant enough. Exercise and hope are essential for everyone. How can you ever know what's possible if you don't try? If stem cell research ever leads to a cure for spinal cord regeneration, people must be physically prepared to move again. And hope—hope is the most potent medicine of all. Taking that away from someone should be a crime.

When I heard that Christopher Reeve had passed away, it brought me to my knees. I will never forget that moment—Superman was gone. I grieved for his wife, his children, and for all of us who saw him as a symbol of strength and perseverance. His death also terrified me. Like so many with severe disabilities, his life was cut short. He had a world-class team caring for him, yet it still wasn't enough. And then there was Brian, who had already outlived Christopher's post-accident years. Unlike Christopher, Brian didn't suffer from respiratory issues, but he also didn't have a medical team. He saw a doctor once a year to renew prescriptions and check his bladder. That was it. It was just me. I was his team.

Chapter Fourteen
When the Screams Wouldn't Stop

In the fall of 2004, I was jolted awake in the middle of the night by the most horrifying sound I had ever heard—Zoe screamed. It was a piercing, gut-wrenching shriek, as if he had been hit by a car. I shot up in bed, my heart pounding.

"ZOE!" I shouted.

He was lying on his side, his head arched backward, legs stretched out stiffly, his body rigid with tension. The terrible screech went on for what felt like an eternity, then, just as suddenly as it started, it stopped. His tongue slipped from his mouth—it was blue. He had wet the bed. I was hysterical. He was limp. My baby was gone.

"No, no, no!" I sobbed, cradling him, stroking his fur, repeating his name over and over, as if saying it could bring him back. I didn't know what to do. I carried him to the living room and gently laid him on the couch, kissing him, willing him to wake up. In my panic, I called my parents. When they finally picked up, all I could manage to say was, "My baby died! My baby died!"

My mom, startled and half-asleep, thought I meant Brian. "Call 911!" she said in a panic.

"No," I choked out, "it's Zoe."

I was out of my mind. But then—Zoe took a deep, shaky breath. His little body shuddered, and he moved his head slightly.

"He's alive!" I gasped into the phone.

My parents said they were on their way. I hung up and frantically called the vet, but the answering service was no help. The woman on the other end told me I would have to wait until the office opened at 7 a.m. So, I sat there, Zoe resting on the couch, my hand gently stroking his head, trying to calm him—trying to calm myself. My parents arrived as quickly as they could. There was nothing we could do until morning, but at least I wasn't alone. They held Zoe while I changed the bedding and got Brian up. His eyes were filled with worry, mirroring my own. None of us knew what had just happened, but one thing was sure—something was terribly wrong.

The vet couldn't do much for Zoe. After a thorough examination, he found nothing obviously wrong aside from extreme exhaustion. He suspected Zoe had suffered a grand mal seizure. There were anti-seizure medications available, but given Zoe's heart condition, the vet didn't recommend them. Instead, he advised me to monitor him closely and sent us home. And monitor him, I did. I barely slept, haunted by the horrific sound of his scream. The memory of it still lingers. Not knowing what had caused the seizure meant I had no way of preventing another one.

Only a couple of weeks later, it happened again. That same piercing cry jolted us awake—another seizure. This time, I was slightly calmer. I gently stroked his chest, watching his shallow breathing. It took a long time for him to take a breath, so I lightly blew into his nose. Suddenly, he snorted and gasped for a deep breath. His head shook as if trying to shake off the episode, then he began panting heavily. Unlike the first time, I didn't call my parents in a panic. Instead, I held him close, comforting him the best I could. I carried him outside for some fresh air, then gave him a warm bath. The seizures left him completely drained. For the rest of the day, he was weak and lethargic, his little body exhausted from the ordeal.

After a few more seizures, I decided to switch veterinarians. I found the only vet in town with an EKG machine, hoping for better insight into Zoe's condition. To my surprise, her primary concern wasn't the seizures—it was his teeth. She explained that his dental issues were affecting his heart, making them an even greater risk than the anesthesia required for surgery. I told her that our previous vet had advised against any procedures, fearing Zoe's age and heart condition made anesthesia too dangerous. At 13 and a half years old, I had to consider every risk carefully. She assured me that during the procedure, Zoe would be closely monitored. If at any point his heart showed signs of distress, she would stop immediately. There were no guarantees, but ignoring the problem wasn't an option. His quality of life was at stake. My belief had always been quality over quantity, and once again, life was testing that philosophy. I had to try.

His surgery was scheduled for early Friday morning. Later that afternoon, Brian had a doctor's appointment. The vet understood Zoe's extreme separation anxiety and hoped he'd be able to go home the same night. That morning, my mom stayed with Brian while I drove Zoe to his appointment. My heart was heavy with the fear that this could be our last day together. How could I say goodbye to this little soul who had been my most faithful friend? Did he know how much I loved him? Did he understand the depth of my gratitude—for all he had given Brian and me? I told him every single day. I tried my best to show him. I wasn't sure how we would have survived those years without him. He had been my anchor, my comfort when I felt utterly alone, even when I thought God Himself had forgotten me.

How do you ever thank someone for loving you so completely?

The vet met us at the front desk, offering a reassuring smile as she tried to ease my worries. She promised to call as soon as the surgery was over. With one last kiss—hoping and praying it wouldn't be the last—I handed Zoe over and walked away, my heart heavy. I had to push my fears aside and focus on getting Brian to his doctor's appointment. Just before we saw the urologist, the vet called. Zoe had made it through the surgery just fine. She had pulled ten teeth, but he was stable and resting in recovery. Relief washed over me. I couldn't imagine how he'd manage with so many teeth missing, but none of that mattered—he was alive.

With that reassurance, Brian and I proceeded to his appointment. His chronic bladder issues had plagued him for years, but now they had reached a critical point. The exams revealed extensive damage, requiring further testing—possibly surgery. I felt like we could never catch a break. How much could one person take? It seemed like every battle we fought was met with another just waiting around the corner.

When Brian—the love of my life—first got sick in June of 1990, my heart began breaking, slowly and steadily, piece by piece. I tried to find joy in Zoe's recovery instead of drowning in the weight of Brian's declining health. And Zoe, despite everything, seemed to have a new lease on life. Once the anesthesia wore off, it was like we had our little puppy back. The infection and plaque buildup had taken such a toll on him that I hadn't even realized how much energy he had lost. Now, with a clean and healthy mouth, his spunk returned.

The vet sent him home with a bottle of pills—small doses of Valium. She explained that if I noticed any signs of an impending seizure, I should give him half a pill to help relax him and, hopefully, prevent another episode. But the seizures continued. And each time, that same gut-wrenching, haunting screech tore through the night.

I almost never slept.

***

In March, I took Brian to see a specialist in Denver for his bladder issues. My mom was in Omaha with Susan as she recovered from surgery, so my dad agreed to help me with the trip. It was a four-hour drive each way, and I knew it wouldn't be an easy appointment. Deep down, I already knew the news wouldn't be good.

I had always understood how fragile life was and how quickly everything could change. Not just from hearing clichés or because someone told me, but because I had lived it. I had experienced that uncertainty firsthand. That understanding made me treasure every single day I had with my boys.

The drive to Denver felt long and tense. With each passing mile, my anxiety grew. I was sweating bullets by the time we arrived. My dad stayed in the van with Zoe while I took Brian inside.

Before the exam, the doctor came in to discuss the procedure. He was young, and almost immediately, he started talking about surgery as if it were inevitable. He didn't just explain the medical aspects—he launched into how much time I would save each day if I didn't have to worry about Brian's catheter. He casually mentioned that with all that newfound free time, I could get a job. There were plenty of trained professionals, he assured me, who could take care of Brian so I wouldn't have to.

Once again, a doctor completely disregarded my role in Brian's life. It was as if it were incomprehensible to him that I not only wanted to care for Brian but that I found deep purpose in doing so. This was our life. No job, no paycheck could ever justify taking time away from the most important thing I would ever do. We clearly didn't share the same values.

I felt insulted but was too preoccupied with the procedure itself to argue. Still, it was disturbing how easily people dismissed my life's work. Money isn't the only reward. No job could ever bring the same sense of purpose, fulfillment, or joy. And beyond that, even if I had wanted to work, the system made it nearly impossible. Unless I made an astronomical salary, enough to pay for all of Brian's care out of pocket, my income would disqualify him from Medicaid and

Medicare. The way the system was structured, it didn't just keep people in poverty—it actively discouraged them from trying to change their circumstances.

The exam Brian needed before surgery involved using a scope to get a live video of the inside of his bladder. It was an outpatient procedure with no sedation. We transferred him to a chair similar to one used in a gynecologist's office, positioning his feet in stirrups and spreading his legs as far apart as possible. The doctor inserted a tube into his urethra, guiding it up to his bladder. Inside the tube was a small camera, and beside us stood a large monitor displaying the live feed.

Then, I saw it.

There it was, clear as day. Cancer. I didn't need the doctor to say a word; I knew. I had never seen a tumor before, but some things you recognize instantly. It was the reason Brian had been so exhausted, the reason he had been slipping away. That cancer had been growing inside him for years, slowly draining the life from him.

The doctor explained that he couldn't take a biopsy at that moment because Brian would need to be sedated for the procedure. But he didn't need to confirm it for me. He also told me that removing Brian's bladder wasn't optional—it was necessary. As he kept talking, explaining the sixteen-hour surgery to remove the bladder and reconstruct a new one from his intestine, I barely heard a word. My mind was spinning. All I wanted was to get Brian home.

I knew, deep in my heart, that this was it. The love of my life was dying. I couldn't put him through months of brutal treatments— surgery, chemotherapy, endless hospital stays—just for the chance at a little more time. Quality over quantity. He had been through enough.

I wheeled Brian out to the van and looked at my dad. "Brian has cancer," I told him.

The drive home was long and quiet, the dark, winding roads stretching ahead of us. All I could think about was getting back to the safety and comfort of home.

Even though the tumor was clearly visible during the scope procedure, the doctor wanted to perform a biopsy to confirm it was malignant. It was a relatively simple and non-invasive procedure that could be performed at our local hospital. Since the tumor was inside Brian's bladder, the doctor could access it easily through a catheter.

But I didn't need a biopsy to tell me what I already knew. As we left the specialist's office in Denver, I was certain that it was cancer. Even if, by some miracle, it wasn't malignant, Brian's bladder was in such poor condition, and the tumor was already obstructing it. Reconstructive surgery was the only option. I felt the pressure from the doctor and scheduled the procedure with the urologist. Brian would need to be put under anesthesia, but it was an outpatient surgery. More than anything, I wanted to make sure Brian never had to spend another night in a hospital again. Still, the thought of anesthesia worried me. Given his neurological damage, the risks were higher. The doctors spoke about the procedure as though it were routine, but they didn't love Brian the way I did. To them, he was just another patient. To me, he was my world.

Meanwhile, my mom was still in Omaha, helping Susan recover from her surgery. Thankfully, she was doing well, which was a huge relief. But I couldn't shake the guilt. I wanted to be there for her the way she had always been there for Brian and me, yet I couldn't. Of course, she understood, but it didn't make me feel any less torn.

Worry consumed me. I worried about Susan. I worried about Zoe, who continued to have seizures. And now, Brian had bladder cancer. The weight of it all pressed down on me until I could barely breathe.

I spoke openly and honestly with Brian about the procedure, wanting him to understand what was ahead and to assure him that I would be by his side every step of the way. He wouldn't have to spend a minute longer in the hospital than necessary—I would take care of him no matter what. I prayed endlessly, pleading with God not to let him suffer.

My dad agreed to look after Zoe for the day so we wouldn't have to worry about him. I knew it would be a long and exhausting ordeal. In the small cubicle before surgery, they sedated Brian. Because of his muscle tightness, he needed to be completely under for the procedure. He hated hospitals—just the sight of one made him anxious. Even the simplest procedures, like a blood draw, would unsettle him. No matter how much I tried to comfort him, his body betrayed his distress. He would shake his arm, cry out, and tremble. Seeing him so upset, unable to calm him, broke me.

For the biopsy, he was positioned in a chair that resembled the ones used in childbirth. The doctor inserted a catheter into his bladder to collect a sample. I kissed Brian a million times, whispering my love over and over. I tried to stay strong, to hold myself together as they wheeled him away, but inside, I was falling apart.

I brought a book to pass the time, but no words seemed to register. My eyes moved across the pages, yet my mind was elsewhere, consumed with worry. Waiting was unbearable. I would have gladly taken his place, enduring any pain to spare him from it. I watched the clock, feeling each passing second stretch into eternity. It was taking longer than expected. Anxiety churned inside me. I called my family to keep them updated. Just as I thought I couldn't stand another moment, the doctor finally called me in.

The urologist, a middle-aged man with the demeanor of a rancher rather than a doctor, spoke awkwardly, mumbling in a way that made it difficult to understand. But one thing was clear—he had torn Brian's urethra during the procedure. Brian was bleeding heavily and would have to stay in the hospital overnight. My heart dropped. I nearly fainted. I had promised Brian he would never have to stay in a hospital again. I instantly regretted this entire procedure. Did it really matter whether we confirmed it was cancer? I already knew.

I demanded to see Brian immediately. They told me he was in recovery and would be moved to a hospital room soon. I called my dad and told him we wouldn't be going home that night. He asked if he should come, and without hesitation, I said yes. Panic rushed through me, overwhelming and suffocating. I needed to see Brian—right now.

I hurried to the unit where they said he'd be, pacing anxiously. I approached the nurses' station, telling them I was waiting for my husband. They barely acknowledged me, too busy with their routine to see my desperation. I watched the elevator, praying for this nightmare to end. No one told me when Brian was moved. They took him through a different hallway, out of my sight. When I finally found his room, only after pressing the staff relentlessly, I walked straight into a scene that shattered me.

There he was, thin and fragile, lying helplessly in a hospital bed. At that moment, I saw him as others did—my poor Brian. I ran to his side, covering him in kisses and tears, my love pouring out of me. I ordered the nurses to step aside. I needed to get him comfortable. I also needed to see the extent of the damage the doctor had done. Though hesitant, the nurses seemed almost relieved to let me take over. They didn't know how to care for him. Brian, still under the effects of anesthesia, was only half-conscious. Blood-soaked gauze was packed around his groin. I demanded that the doctor come to the room. Staying the night was not an option.

I had never handled blood well, but I would figure out how to care for him at home if it meant getting him out of that hospital. I wasn't asking—I was telling the doctor. The sterile smell, the beeping machines, the stark white walls—it was too much. My body reacted violently. My knees went weak, my stomach lurched, and I vomited several times. My entire being screamed to get out of there.

After speaking with the doctor, he agreed that there was nothing they could do for Brian that I couldn't do myself. That was all I needed to hear. I called my dad. I couldn't drive. He had to get us.

Dressing Brian was a struggle. I had to sit down multiple times, dizzy and nauseous. My hands trembled as I fastened each button, my only focus on getting him out of that room. I asked the aide for help, not because I needed it, but because I wanted to leave as quickly as possible. We didn't belong there. We just needed to go home.

The moment we stepped outside, I felt a wave of relief. I tilted Brian's chair back as far as possible, placed his neck pillow around him, and let him rest for the drive home. We were leaving it all behind; no more hospitals, no more doctors, no more nurses.

Once we got home, I settled Brian into bed and took a long shower. I needed to wash away the grime, the weight of everything we had just endured. As the hot water poured over me, I felt some of the tension ease, but anger quickly took its place. I was furious at the doctor for being so careless, for causing Brian unnecessary pain. A simple procedure shouldn't have resulted in such trauma.

For the next week, Brian had to use an indwelling catheter. His groin was swollen, bruised, and bloodied. Every time I washed him, I cried. Why did it have to be this way? I hated myself for going through with the procedure. But I clung to one small consolation: I had kept my promise. Brian would never have to spend another night in the hospital again.

The biopsy results came back almost immediately. It was cancer.

Chapter Fifteen
The Final Goodbye

T he urologist referred us to a specialist in Denver to discuss our options. Once again, the only option presented was surgery, removing the tumor, along with Brian's entire bladder. They would also take part of his intestine to create a conduit from his kidneys through his abdominal wall to a stoma. The surgery would take at least 16 grueling hours, carrying enormous risks. Most patients suffered severe depression and complications afterward. Brian would have to spend weeks in the hospital, followed by months of rehabilitation, along with radiation or chemotherapy.

It was too much. We couldn't even survive one night in the hospital. How could we endure months? I knew deep in my heart we couldn't. We wouldn't.

I told the doctor we wouldn't be moving forward with the surgery. The next step was to meet with an oncologist to set up hospice care. I had no idea why we even needed this appointment—Brian's primary care doctor could have handled it. It felt like another pointless hurdle, another round of waiting in sterile rooms for something that should have been simple.

We sat in the waiting room. Then in the exam room. Waiting again, just for a prescription.

A nurse came in and reached for a thermometer. I stopped her. "Brian doesn't like that in his ear," I told her. He didn't have a fever anyway. Then she pulled out a blood pressure cuff. I cut her off again. "No." Restraints of any kind made Brian anxious, and if she wanted to see his blood pressure rise, trying to strap his arm was the fastest way to do it. What did it even matter now? He was dying. I told her to leave us alone. We'd just wait for the doctor.

When the oncologist finally walked in, he didn't even look at Brian. Didn't speak to him. Didn't acknowledge him at all. Typical. Instead, he turned to me and said, "You're doing the right thing."

What?

Don't talk to me. You don't know me. I wasn't here for your validation or your opinion. I just needed a prescription to start hospice care. I bit my tongue, said as little as possible, took the paper, and left.

As soon as we got home, I called hospice. A nurse came out with the paperwork. I needed to know everything—how this would happen, what to expect, how Brian would die. I had to prepare myself. There wasn't much they could do except manage his pain and answer my questions. I read everything they gave me.

Then I sat with Brian and told him how sorry I was. Sorry that life had cheated him. Sorry that he would never get the ending he deserved. But I never gave up on him. I loved him, no matter what. Whether he could speak or not, I would be with him every step of the way. Just like our song—*After all, I will be the one to hold you in my arms*. I would not let him down.

I prayed. I screamed. I begged.

I was so frustrated with God. I couldn't believe I'd never hear Brian's voice again. I didn't understand. *Why, Brian? Why? Why? Why?*

Sometimes, I screamed at the sky, fists clenched, demanding answers that never came.

All I could do now was hope—if there was something beyond this life—that Brian would be free. That he would be happy. That, wherever he was going, he would be safe and loved.

I couldn't bring myself to call his mom, so I wrote her a letter instead. I told her I didn't know how much time Brian had left, but it wouldn't be long. She called after reading it. Our conversation was difficult. We had never truly formed a bond over the years. She said she would call often to check in on us.

Later, Brian's youngest sister called. She wanted to say goodbye. She told me she had a baby boy now and wanted to drive down for a few days with her in-laws, since she needed help with the baby. Their mother wanted to come too. I thought it would be good for Brian to see his family one last time. But part of me bristled when she said she needed help. For sixteen years, it had never once occurred to her that I might have needed help too. That bitterness could have eaten a hole in my soul if I let it, but I had to let it go.

By then, Brian slept most of the day. I used a travel pillow to support his head in his chair so he could rest comfortably without having to stay in bed all day. By June, I stopped using the Easy Stand. It had simply become too much for him.

For sixteen years, I had fought for Brian's recovery. Every single day, I stretched his muscles, stood him up, and tried to get him to speak. I *never* gave up. Letting go of that fight—accepting that hope was no longer enough—was one of the hardest things I had ever done.

I still stretched him so he wouldn't be uncomfortable, but I stopped using the wedge. The pressure on his stomach was too much. Most days, we just lie together on the futon—Brian, Zoe, and me. They were my world. They were the reason I got up every day. And I was losing them both.

My sisters came to visit at the beginning of July, knowing it would be the last time they would see Brian. It was heart-wrenching—almost unbearable to experience, let alone to remember.

Later that month, Brian's sister, her baby—Brian's nephew—her in-laws, and their mother came for a short visit. Despite the past tensions, I knew Brian loved his family, and I wanted him to see them one last time. His nephew looked exactly like Brian's baby pictures. Brian smiled often while watching him, and I couldn't help but wonder if this was what our son might have looked like. All those years of wishing we had a child together...

When they left, I felt relieved. As Brian's mother hugged me goodbye, she whispered two unexpected words: *"Thank you."*

Watching Brian slip away was excruciating. And just when I thought I had reached my limit, I received more devastating news. In early August, wildfires tore through the Nebraska Panhandle, consuming our family home in Chadron—the house my father built. Though we hadn't lived there in years, it was *home*. Every piece of wood had my father's fingerprints on it. Every nail, every screw was placed by his hands. That house held more than walls—it held our childhood, our memories, our dreams. It was where Brian and I fell in love. It was where we exchanged our wedding vows. Now, it was gone, reduced to ash and lost forever.

I was grateful that my mom visited every day, spending time with us whether we were sitting outside or watching TV together. Brian slept most of the day, but when he was awake, he seemed content. In fact, I even told the hospice nurse not to come until I called her—her visits felt like an unwelcome reminder of the inevitable, as if she were waiting for Brian to pass away. I hated that feeling, so I preferred to delay her visits until absolutely necessary.

On Friday, August 18th, Brian's pain escalated dramatically. Although he had shown signs of blood in his urine for a while, he remained relatively comfortable—until that morning. At our usual 6:30 start, I got him up, made coffee and breakfast, and ensured he took his morning pill to activate his muscle relaxer, as his legs had grown painfully tight from prolonged bed rest. After our routine shower and getting him dressed, we set out in the van for grocery shopping. Suddenly, Brian began moaning in distress. Alarmed, I drove home immediately, gave him a strong painkiller, adjusted his neck pillow, and called his doctor—then I called hospice.

I trusted my instincts; I knew this level of pain meant I needed help. Although it had only been three weeks since I'd canceled hospice services, I was relieved for that brief respite. Soon after, a hospice nurse arrived. I needed someone to guide me in making Brian more comfortable. As we sat together at the dining room table, I was shocked when the nurse remarked that if he were in Brian's condition—not as a cancer patient but as a disabled person—he wouldn't want to live that way. Such comments, echoing a sentiment I've heard too often about life "like that," felt like an accusation that I should have let him go long ago. I refused to accept that notion; Brian had survived his illness, and I would never consider ending his life. What are we supposed to do—abandon or even end the lives of people who live with disabilities? That isn't care; it's murder. I felt as if that nurse was implying I had been wrong to care for Brian, and that I should have let him die long ago. Such a cold, twisted philosophy is beyond comprehension. Brian survived his illness; he didn't die. Was I really expected to let him go? I can't fathom a mindset that devalues the lives of those who need care and compassion the most. And even worse, hearing this from a health care provider.

The nurse then inserted an indwelling catheter into Brian's bladder to more effectively drain the urine and blood, explaining that the tumor was likely growing and could eventually block his bladder, leading to kidney failure and complete shutdown. Terrified at the thought of further suffering, I signed the necessary paperwork, and he reassured me he'd return after his 9 o'clock meeting on Monday.

That night, overwhelmed with fear and sorrow, I held onto hope that we would find a way to ease his pain without losing the precious time we had left together. As the nurse was leaving, my mom arrived and promised to stay, even though it was only mid-afternoon. I helped Brian get up so he could have a bite to eat and sit in the living room instead of staying in bed. Even though he wasn't very hungry, I placed him on the couch, as I did every night after dinner. After receiving his terminal cancer diagnosis, I tried to keep up our routine until Brian told me it was too much for him. Lying on the futon with his feet on the floor, he looked more at ease—able to watch TV, listen to conversation, and enjoy Zoe's gentle licks on his face.

That night, despite drinking plenty of fluids, his output was low, and I hoped the extra water might flush out his bladder and help clear the blood. Although he was comfortable on the couch, I eventually moved him to bed. Our nightly routine had always been intimate—like our mornings together. Every night, I undressed him, carefully tended to his skin, combed his hair, trimmed his nails, and massaged lotion into his feet. I kissed his face and whispered how much I loved him until he drifted off. Most nights, I would fall asleep with him by my side and our little dog nearby, filling me with comfort and love. But that Friday, I couldn't sleep. Brian seemed particularly uncomfortable, and I feared something was wrong with his catheter—his leg bag remained empty. At midnight, I woke my mom and called the nurse, even though I dreaded doing so. The on-call nurse, Mayda, promised to come over right away. With the windows open for fresh air, my mom and Zoe kept vigil by the window as I sat with Brian.

When Mayda arrived, she suspected a blockage in the catheter, possibly a blood clot, but didn't have the supplies to flush his bladder immediately, so she had to go to the hospital. Meanwhile, Brian's discomfort worsened, and I administered extra pain medication. He began moaning a low, unfamiliar sound that broke my heart. Every minute of waiting felt like an eternity.

By mid-afternoon, after some desperate attempts with Mayda to flush his bladder, I gave Brian a quick shower before returning him to bed. I didn't even try transferring him into his wheelchair. Instead, Mayda showed me how to use an eyedropper to give him small doses of morphine and Valium—medications that, although effective, brought back painful memories of his extended hospital stay in France. I gave him these drops every few hours to stay ahead of the pain, and I was relieved to see him relax a little. However, I soon noticed his breathing became irregular—eerily reminiscent of the time he was in a coma nearly sixteen years ago to the day.

I told the nurse that evening that I feared he was slipping into a coma, and she agreed. I re-read the hospice pamphlet about the final stages of life and realized with a crushing certainty that this was it— my love was dying. Each irregular breath made me worry it might be his last. I never imagined I would lose him; I could endure anything as long as he was by my side. In desperation, I begged, "Please don't leave me! You are the love of my life." I kissed every inch of his face, hands, and feet, pleading for him to stay, knowing that his talent, gentleness, kindness, and beauty were irreplaceable.

That Sunday night, Brian held on, his skin pale and almost translucent. I gently washed his face with a soft washcloth, savoring every tender touch. To fill the quiet, I played his old recordings—the soulful compilations of his saxophone performances and singing that once brought us so much joy. We listened together, lost in memories of happier times. Even Zoe, usually so lively, stayed away from the room, perhaps too overwhelmed to join our farewell.

My mom kept vigil at the foot of his bed all night, and by morning, my dad helped adjust the bed to make Brian more comfortable. Susan called from Omaha, and I held the phone to his ear so he could hear her voice. Through tears, she told him how much she loved him and that he was her brother. The moment was unbearably sad.

Brian was 45—so beautiful, so easy to love, the center of my world. I met him when I was 18, and 18 years later, I was saying goodbye. I wasn't ready to let go. "Brian, don't you ever forget me!" I pleaded, whispering, "I love you," even though words felt so inadequate in that moment. How do you speak to the love of your life on his deathbed, when all you can do is hold his hand as he slips away?

Just as he had promised after his 9 o'clock meeting, the nurse arrived. I asked him to help me gently turn Brian to make him more comfortable, though his body no longer responded as it once had over our sixteen years together. With the draw sheet in hand, we carefully repositioned him, and in that quiet, fateful moment, Brian was gone.

The nurse tapped my shoulder gently, urging me to look as Brian opened his eyes one last time. And then, with that final, silent farewell, his spirit left this world.

Everything after Brian died is a blur. The nurse gave me a moment alone with him. I kissed him, told him I loved him one last time, but I knew—his soul had already left. I was sure of it. It had been nearly eighteen years to the day since we first met—half my lifetime.

My mom came in to say goodbye, then my dad. Zoe refused to enter the room. He was acting strange. I couldn't process it. I just knew I couldn't be the one to call Brian's mother. I couldn't tell her that her firstborn son was gone. The nurse made the call for me. He also helped me dress Brian one last time. My sisters were coming the next day and wanted to see him at the funeral home before he was cremated. I needed help—something I hadn't needed in a long time. His body didn't feel like his. It was stiff, foreign. I sobbed as I dressed him, moaning in pain that I thought would kill me. I wished it would. I couldn't understand how I was still alive when I hurt that badly. But I did it—I dressed my husband one last time. His nice slacks, a button-up white shirt. He looked handsome. He always did—my love.

I was glad I had made Brian's final arrangements earlier. We had decided long ago that we wanted to be cremated. With the Teacher's Retirement Fund that I had cashed out, I'd already paid for it. I didn't want a funeral. I celebrated Brian's life every single day. And honestly, I didn't know who would have come anyway. We lived in a tiny, remote town. I was relieved I had made the arrangements before his cancer diagnosis. It was one less thing to carry.

When the funeral home arrived, the nurse told me it would be best if I didn't watch. He thought it would be too much. I could barely stand. But I couldn't look away. I watched them enter our bedroom with the stretcher. I had never let anyone move Brian without me. I was terrified they'd hurt him. Even now, even in death, I worried they would drop him.

Then they rolled the stretcher through the house, out to the van. When I saw his face covered with a sheet, I wailed. He would suffocate! Oh God—he was dead. The weight of it crushed me.

The nurse sat beside me, trying to calm me.

"What do I do now?" I asked.

"What do you mean? Do you want me to call someone?"

"No... What am I supposed to do now?"

Silence. There was nothing to do.

For sixteen years, every moment of my life had revolved around Brian's care—making his lunch, getting his pills, transferring him, sitting him up, laying him down. Now, there was nothing. No purpose. No direction. Nothing.

That evening, my mom and I went for a walk while we waited for Susan. She had left work the moment she heard, one last time, she made the long trip across the state for Brian.

It was the first time we stepped outside without him. I tried to walk Zoe, but he was grieving too. He wouldn't move. So, I carried him. But there was no wheelchair to hang his bag on. That realization nearly broke me.

Where would Zoe sit now? How would I carry him everywhere? Oh God—how was I supposed to go on?

Susan arrived, and together we wept, our grief pouring out in waves. That night, for the first time in 16 years, I slept alone. Zoe refused to enter the bedroom—my poor little guy was devastated. I was, too. But I had nothing left in me to comfort him. I was utterly spent. The only reason I managed to sleep was sheer exhaustion. I sobbed until I nearly vomited. Finally, I laid one of Brian's sweaters on his side of the bed and pretended he was still there.

I arranged with the hospice to have all of Brian's equipment removed from our home as quickly as possible. I donated his wheelchair, hospital bed, Hoyer lift, shower/commode chair, wedge, Easy Stand, and other supplies to hospice and the Veterans' Home, knowing that someone else could benefit from them. I discarded his medications, bedding, and urinary products because I couldn't bear to look at his empty wheelchair or hold his pillow any longer. It was time to let go. I knew I had to move. I couldn't stay in a house without Brian, and that town offered no future for me. Although I wasn't sure what the next chapter would bring, I was determined to start anew. The next day, Georgia and Liz flew in from the East Coast and helped me pack, even organizing an impromptu yard sale to sell some of our belongings.

On Wednesday morning, Susan, Georgia, and Liz went to the funeral home to say goodbye to Brian, while my parents and I had already said our farewells at home. Liz was hesitant about seeing him after he had passed, but I convinced her that experiencing that moment would bring the closure she needed. When they returned, their faces were somber, yet they said he looked peaceful, and they were glad they had gone. Shortly thereafter, he was cremated, and his ashes arrived the next day. Now, the remains of the love of my life are confined to a small box—a haunting reminder that I carry with me for the rest of my days.

At Susan's suggestion, we created a unique memorial for Brian. We each wrote a heartfelt note—my personal message, "I will always love you, Brian"—and tied them to balloons that we released one by one from the top of Scottsbluff Monument. I hope he knew just how deeply we all loved him. My dear friend Mary drove across the state the moment she heard the news; she didn't hesitate to come—she just did, and that meant the world to me. Many friends reached out with calls and cards, a testament to how many lives Brian touched.

In the following months, Zoe's behavior grew increasingly erratic. He refused to enter the bedroom, and his seizures became more frequent, turning every night into a living nightmare. I tried sleeping on the living room floor with him, but nothing alleviated the sorrow. Meanwhile, my sisters helped me pack and store our belongings while I wrestled with our next steps. Eventually, Zoe and I stayed at my parents' house for a month until we moved to Missoula, Montana—a small mountain town my parents had once mentioned. I longed for a fresh start in a beautiful, new place where I could finally embrace the outdoors, as Brian and I had always dreamed. I even promised Brian that I would live in the mountains.

Yet, I was plagued by worry about Zoe. His nightly seizures continued, his heart medication was prohibitively expensive, and his grief mirrored my own. I even agonized over the possibility of euthanizing him, tormented by the thought of losing my little companion. My parents urged me to hold on, reminding me of the comfort and love Zoe brought into my life. Reluctantly, I decided to wait.

So, we set out for Montana. I found a pet-friendly apartment and a job, and my mom stayed with us for the first two months to help care for Zoe—an essential support as I faced the daunting challenge of moving on without her. I agonized for months over how I would manage Zoe's care on my own. In our new home, everything was different. Zoe missed his familiar routine—he was not used to being alone for hours, without his favorite spot or his bag to snuggle in. His nights were filled with anxiety, and he continued to experience seizures. The thought of watching him suffer further was unbearable.

Finally, on a cold December day, I made the appointment I'd been dreading. With a heavy heart, I held my little boy one last time. He trembled with nervousness, and I felt like an executioner. I couldn't believe it had come to this; losing the two loves of my life felt unimaginable. I carefully clipped a few strands of Zoe's hair to keep, inhaling his familiar scent and silently praying for his forgiveness.

As I cradled him on my lap, the vet prepared to administer the injection. I whispered, "Give Brian kisses for me," knowing that this final act was borne of pure love, even as it shattered my heart.

Chapter Sixteen
When You Wish Upon a Star

O ne of the things that frustrates me most is when people assume I want their pity. When asked how I'm doing, I've heard things like, "I just feel terrible for you, you poor thing." I never knew how to respond. Usually, I said nothing, caught off guard by the words. Throughout the years of caring for Brian, I heard similar comments, and no matter how many times it happened, it always unsettled me. I'm not quick with words, and sometimes I'm so taken aback that I can't even process why someone would say such things. Unfortunately, those words stick with me. It's not that I care what people think of me or my life—I want them to understand something, pity is a terrible thing, and I don't want their pity. What people think they're pitying is a misunderstanding. Yes, what happened to Brian was devastating. I wouldn't wish it on anyone; losing his physical abilities and his voice was an unimaginable loss. I grieved deeply for the life he had had before he got sick. But Brian was loved. He lived a life full of meaning, joy, and connection. And as for me, I suffered an enormous loss, too. I lost the future we had dreamed of, our goals, and life as we knew it. But despite it all, we had so much to celebrate. Our lives had depth and meaning. Our extraordinary love carried us through challenges most people will never understand. Even without words, we found ways to communicate. And somehow, after everything, Brian was still so lovable—perhaps even more so.

Loving and caring for Brian was the greatest gift of my life. In many ways, he became like an infant, someone you love unconditionally, without hesitation. Providing for him gave me a profound sense of purpose and fulfillment. I know I will never find anything more meaningful than my role as his caregiver. No job, no amount of money, and no societal expectation could ever compare to the depth of what I did for Brian. People may have thought I sacrificed so much, but I don't see it that way. I made a choice—an unwavering commitment—to give Brian the best life possible. And I take enormous pride in that.

I didn't just care for him—I immersed myself in learning everything I could to help him thrive. I studied physical therapy, occupational therapy, recreational therapy, and speech therapy. I learned massage, reflexology, nutrition—whatever it took to improve his life and mine. And I applied that knowledge every single day. Because of that, Brian never had a bedsore, never fell, was never dropped, never left alone, and after his initial illness, never had to be hospitalized under my care.

Life is hard. Sometimes unbearably so. People tell me I should embrace this newfound freedom as if I've been given a gift. Even my father said that I'm finally part of the "real world" again. In a way, he's right—I'm living in the real world, but without the love of my life. A world where my happiness came from looking into Brian's eyes and finding solace no longer exists. Those who believe this could be a fresh start for me don't understand. They see my life through their perspective, not mine. They saw the challenges—Brian's disability, and the sacrifices I made to care for him. They saw what I gave up. Maybe they only saw the hardships. But what they didn't see—or perhaps couldn't comprehend—was that I found joy in that life. It may be difficult for some to understand, but I love caring for him. I love celebrating the lives of those I love. I found purpose in the daily routines, the small gestures, the quiet moments of connection. I cherished the life Brian and I had, not despite its challenges, but because of the love that filled it.

I loved Brian in a way that I don't think most people can fathom. And now, I miss him in a way that words can't fully capture. I miss caring for him. I miss kissing him. I miss the smell of his skin, the sound of his laughter, the way his eyes lit up when I sang to him in the shower. I miss cooking for him, shopping for him, washing his clothes. I even miss cutting his hair and the scent of his shaving cream. I miss *everything.*

And what do I have now? No one. No purpose. Life isn't meant to be this lonely. It isn't supposed to feel so empty. How am I supposed to endure a life that's now just about *existing*—until when? Until I die? What if that's years from now? Every breath I take feels like it's pulling me further away from him.

People should have known—my refusal to even consider putting Brian in a nursing home should have been enough to show them. I wanted Brian and me to live in the *real* world. I don't believe in pushing people aside because they're different or need extra care. Our life together was real. It was full. It was *ours.* And now, I don't know how to exist without it.

People say the oddest things to me. One of the most common is, *"You're an angel."* That phrase has always bothered me. It makes me out to be something more than human, something otherworldly. But I'm not. I'm no angel. I'm just a woman who, when faced with impossible circumstances, rose to meet them. I had the same needs and desires as everyone else. I didn't do anything that any one of us *couldn't* do—I just *did it.*

So many people place their loved ones in institutions because they say they *have to.* But I was capable. I was willing. I had the determination to do whatever it took to keep Brian at home, to give him the best life I could. Yes, we were broke—so broke that we didn't even qualify for Habitat for Humanity. So broke that the state wouldn't allow us to keep Brian's retirement fund, forcing us to cash it out early and lose half of it—money that could have helped me survive after he was gone. It felt like society wanted to leave us with nothing. This is the same country where people chant "USA" at sporting events, where politicians and families alike preach about strong family values—yet those values seem to vanish when people like us need help. I was a hard-working, law-abiding American. I lived my values every single day through my love and devotion to Brian. And yet, in the eyes of society, I was invisible. I held no worth.

I'd rather live in poverty than face the only alternative, a nursing home. I could never subject the one I love to that kind of isolation. Society has normalized institutionalizing those who need care simply because caring for family at home is seen as too difficult. I recognize that not everyone can provide full-time care. Many individuals with conditions like dementia or Alzheimer's truly need specialized facilities. But I deliberately chose to care for Brian, honoring our wedding vows by staying with him through sickness and health. Why isn't there more support for families like ours? Often, this approach is not only more compassionate but also more cost-effective than institutional care. We have so many resources in this country—if only wealth were shared in a way that truly valued human life and quality of life. Instead, access to basic healthcare is frequently tied to income, as though illnesses or disabilities were a punishment for not praying hard enough. It's disheartening to hear "Christians" say that if Brian and I had just prayed more, Jesus would heal him—implying our pain is our own failing. That perspective is so far removed from the true message of love and compassion that I can hardly respond.

We no longer value the sacred bonds of family care. Instead, our medical system is driven by class, and the extended family is seen as a burden. Even the doctors and hospice staff downplayed the vital role I played in Brian's care. They suggested I outsource his care so I could focus on paid work, as if my unpaid labor didn't count as real work. I'm in healthcare too, devoted to caring for his well-being. When a hospice nurse remarked that he wouldn't want to live "that way," I was shocked. Did he really think it was a choice? Their suggestion was essentially to hide him away, to prioritize making money over genuine compassion. It felt like they were dismissing our humanity. People with special needs are routinely sent away to institutions because caring for them at home is viewed as too challenging. Even when government assistance is available, it's offered on terms that make it impossible to live on. I know this all too well: when senators balance the budget, they always cut from those who need help the most.

I've written letters to senators, congressmen, governors, and even the president, and protested Medicaid cuts. Yet every year, the most vulnerable are left with fewer resources, and institutional care becomes a default option. I have seen the neglect and loneliness in nursing homes, where residents suffer from pressure sores and are treated like cattle, their dignity stripped away.

For 16 years, I devoted myself to caring for Brian around the clock. As his wife, I vowed to be there for him in sickness and in health, but his need for 24-hour care meant I was on duty every minute, with no holidays, sick days, or vacations. There were no provisions made for my own well-being. With Brian unable to work and me unable to work because I was his caregiver, I struggled to cover even basic expenses like clothing. Society dismissed me as "just a housewife" with no income. Yet, if you truly considered it, you'd see that supporting me to care for Brian is far more cost-effective than institutionalizing him. Every professional—respite care aides, therapists, nurses, doctors—was paid for their work. But what about me? Who cares for the person who gives everything to keep his loved one at home?

I vowed to Brian that I would never let him endure that life. I would rather we both be gone than allow him to live in a place that devalues his worth. Caring for him wasn't just a duty—it was an honor, a privilege, and the most genuine expression of my love.

For sixteen years, our days revolved around the basics. I cooked for Brian, carefully preparing a balanced diet in the hope that good nutrition would reduce our need for doctors—I'd like never to set foot in a hospital again. I made sure he drank plenty of water to keep his kidneys and bladder healthy, and I handled all his bowel and bladder care myself. I'm constantly astonished when I hear new parents complain about being woken in the night to feed or change their baby. How can anyone be so reluctant to sacrifice a little sleep for the care of a precious new life? It seems our society has lost touch with a fundamental truth: mammals are instinctively wired to care for their young. Mothers, in particular, would risk everything to nurture and protect their offspring. We could learn a lot from the natural world about the true value of family and the selfless care it demands.

I took great pride in maintaining Brian's look—his haircut and wardrobe—exactly as he would have wanted. He was a very handsome man, and I wanted him to feel clean, healthy, and normal, despite the unfair stigma that comes with being in a wheelchair. Society often treats people with disabilities differently, and I refused to let Brian suffer from that prejudice. I've heard people justify discrimination in the most absurd ways—like one woman claiming she wouldn't rent to someone with a disability because "they're dirty." And I recall a German instructor at UNL who, in front of me, argued that including students with disabilities in regular classes would detract from her daughter's education. I was both shocked and dismayed by her lack of compassion, and I later wrote her a concise essay reminding her of history's darkest moments—the Nazis' attempt to eliminate those they deemed "other." It still baffles me that, in our modern society, the notion persists that people with special needs are somehow less deserving of care and acceptance.

Someone on the city bus remarked, "How nice it is that they installed a wheelchair lift so you can get out, too." I am grateful for the Americans with Disabilities Act, which helps us avoid being relegated to basements and institutions. Charity should never imply that those who receive help are less than those who give it. Every human life has intrinsic value, and the dignity of those in need must always be respected.

For years, Brian looked perfectly normal to most people, even though he couldn't speak, his facial expressions remained natural, and he never exhibited overt signs of his condition. Yet strangers still stared. Sometimes I'd get so frustrated I'd snap back or stick my tongue out in defiance. I resented it when complete strangers gawked or asked intrusive questions like, "How does he go to the bathroom?" as if I were expected to explain everything about catheters to someone I barely knew. I also hated when strangers offered unsolicited permission, saying things like, "It'd be okay if you chose not to stay with him." It felt as though they were giving themselves an out, just in case our roles were reversed. I never needed anyone's opinion, permission, or absolution. Those people didn't share my experience. They assumed they pitied us, that their prayers for us were more about easing their own guilt— "Thank God that isn't me"—without ever truly understanding our situation or what I had chosen. I wasn't forced to care for Brian; I made that choice at the age of 20, and it remains my proudest achievement. I chose to care for him and to be happy, providing the best life I could for both of us. I treasured every day we spent together—through all the successes, the fun moments we planned, and the trying times as well. When I pledged my love to him on that unforgettable day, September 2, 1989, I meant every word. I had no way of knowing what the future would hold, but I promised to stand by his side until death parted us—and I kept that promise.

I wasn't compensated for my work as a caregiver. Social workers suggested that if I divorced Brian, I might receive payment, but as long as we were married, I wasn't eligible for any financial assistance. While Brian qualified for Medicaid, Medicare, low-income housing, food stamps, and energy support, I did not. We barely scraped by each month, forgoing many things that most people take for granted. I couldn't imagine any conventional job that would fit into the two hours of respite I had each day. Financial worries were a constant burden.

I made a conscious decision early on about how I wanted to live: to spend my days with those I love and to engage in the activities that bring me joy. While many say they value such a life, few truly commit to it. —I chose to make the most of every moment. I found happiness in cooking, baking, cleaning, and creating a warm, welcoming home. Books became my refuge, transporting me to fantastic worlds, and Brian always cherished when I read to him. I used my respite time to run and further my education at the University, and even took Brian to the tennis courts so he could still share in the excitement of watching me hit the ball, even if he could no longer play.

I knew that statistically, someone with Brian's level of disability wasn't likely to live a long life. In the face of inevitable challenges, I found solace in counting my blessings. I've always taken joy in life's simple pleasures. I'm not naïve, but I truly value the little things. When I search for inspiration outside my own life, it's hard to find. I don't envy others; in fact, some of society's most celebrated figures seem utterly monotonous to me. Too many people chase the same material markers of success, repeating the same mistakes, until they lose sight of what once brought them genuine joy. I firmly believe you can tell what a person truly values by how they spend their time and resources—their actions speak far louder than their words.

I do have regrets. I regret that, for so many years, financial constraints made everything so much harder for us. It's absurd that, despite the resources of our families and the government's vast expenditures, we struggled so profoundly. I'm deeply pained by the fact that I suffered health issues simply because I couldn't afford proper medical care. It's heartbreaking that some family members chose to distance themselves instead of offering even a little help, making us feel like a burden. They missed an opportunity to share a small part of their time, money, or support—and in doing so, they lost the chance to experience the grace and dignity that come from doing good. I never expected anyone to sacrifice their dreams for us, but if the roles were reversed, I couldn't imagine watching a loved one struggle without offering help.

Now, I'm left wondering how to fill the emptiness that remains in my life. Grieving is an arduous, ongoing process—one that those around me can only begin to understand. Some people see this newfound "freedom" as a blessing, but for me, it feels crippling. One year after Brian died, I struggled just to keep moving, living through a lonely, forgettable period. I eventually moved to a beautiful mountain town to start anew. I found some solace in the peace and beauty of nature, which helped me endure my inner turmoil and sorrow.

For that year, survival was all I could manage. I barely remember it, and I prefer not to, because if I had stopped moving, I would have crumbled. Even while I pushed forward, there were moments when overwhelming grief would seize me, like when I was out running and a deep, primal moan escaped me, a cry from the very depths of my soul that I couldn't control or silence. No whispered comfort could ease that pain, a pain I know I will carry with me for the rest of my life.

I go on without my husband—my best friend and the love of my life—and without Zoe. I'm left to rebuild who I am, no longer defined as a wife, caregiver, or mother, but as someone striving to become the person Brian would have loved, cherished, and been proud of. I still long for his love; I loved him with every breath, as deeply and truly as any soulmate can. I feel blessed to have experienced that kind of love—a love not measured by material gifts or grand declarations, but proven by our unwavering commitment through sickness and health, in good times and bad. Even when Brian could no longer speak or care for himself, my love for him remained a powerful testament to our bond. I carry on because I know that, despite everything, he loved me too—I could see it in his eyes and feel it in my heart. I was truly loved, and that is something I will always hold dear.

Our love story is unlike any other. When I share our life, I know many won't fully understand—it defies simple explanation. All the love songs and poems I've known speak of limitless love, a love where no mountain is too high and no river too deep to keep me from loving him until the end of time. I believed in that love. I dreamed of it. I lived it. It truly exists, and I want our story to remind others that true love is worth waiting for and worth living for. Our journey is one for the record books, and I'm preserving it so that it endures forever.

Epilogue

It's been almost twenty years since I wrote this memoir when I was living in Missoula, Montana. I worked at a hotel and used their business center computer to write late into the night. Summers in Missoula burst with color and beauty, but the winters were overcast and grey. I knew I was grieving, though I hadn't yet recognized the toll of seasonal affective disorder—I desperately needed sunlight. I was in a very dark place, even contemplating ending my life because the sadness and pain felt unbearable. Society often romanticizes the idea of one spouse dying so soon after the other as a testament to true love, but at 36, I couldn't die, my body was healthy, my heart ached, and I wanted to leave behind the legacy of my love for Brian.

I poured my energy into writing our story, determined to ensure that Brian would never be forgotten, even as my own thoughts drifted toward self-destruction. One night, I had a vivid dream of asphyxiating myself, and I saw Susan and my Mom discovering the devastation I'd caused. I woke, drenched in tears and sweat, unable to bear the thought of hurting them. In that desperate moment, I reached out to my friend Kristy—my lifesaver. She urged me to hold on, promising that if I persisted, things would eventually get better, and that Brian would want me to live. That phone call changed everything. I decided if I wasn't going to die, I was going to live. Unsure exactly what that meant, I resolved to stop wallowing in grief. I applied for my first credit card, bought a computer, and committed to finishing our story. My dad, who wanted nothing more than for me to move forward, was thrilled when I shared my plans.

I was terrified, worried that by moving forward I might seem as if I had forgotten Brian or stopped loving him. I struggled with that thought for a long time, but gradually, I began to look forward rather than dwell on the past. I realized I had to move forward. While Missoula had its beauty, I knew that if I wanted to truly thrive, I needed more sunshine, more mountains, and a place that offered greater opportunities.

I'd never been to Colorado Springs before, but I was drawn to it for its 300-plus days of sunshine and the stunning mountain backdrop to the west. I relocated to Colorado Springs in June 2009, and over time, I've built a community of friends and found fulfilling work here—it's truly become my home.

I think of Brian every single day. Every birthday and anniversary of his passing, I feel like I should do something to honor him—to let him know I'm still thinking of him, still loving him from afar. When I first started writing this memoir, it wasn't just to tell our story. It was meant to be something I left behind. I couldn't bring myself to finish that last chapter. The pain of reliving it, of putting those final words onto paper, was too much. I let it sit for months. Then, after moving to Colorado Springs, I met Tony in June. He became a close friend, someone I trusted. One day, instead of trying to explain my story to him, I handed him my manuscript. Letting him read it was easier than speaking the words out loud. I hadn't proofread it or asked anyone to edit it—it was too raw, too personal. But with Tony, I finally felt safe enough to share it. His reaction changed everything. My story so moved him that he insisted I publish it. For the first time, I considered that maybe my words were worth sharing. I took a copy to a literary agent, hoping for guidance. But months passed, and she never even looked at it—she didn't even remember me when I went back to retrieve it.

Then, something unexpected happened. A copy made its way into the hands of people from our past, and eventually, it reached Mr.

Roger Greenberg from UNC. Our story so touched him that he reached out to me. He encouraged me to establish a memorial scholarship in Brian's name at UNC—something that would carry his legacy forward long after we were gone.

I raised the money, and today, that scholarship stands as a tribute to Brian, ensuring that his name and spirit will live on at UNC for generations to come. UNC hosted a luncheon for the families of Memorial Scholarship namesakes, and I was invited to attend. The event included lunch, a Jazz Band rehearsal, and the opportunity to meet the first recipient of Brian's scholarship. I was honored and deeply proud to see this tribute to Brian come to life.

The drive to Greeley was about an hour and a half, and with each passing mile, my emotions swirled—nervousness, anticipation, and an overwhelming sense of longing. When I arrived, I was warmly welcomed and escorted to the Jazz Band room to observe a rehearsal. As the music filled the space, I bit my lip to hold back tears. Oh, how I had missed this—the energy, the passion, the sound that had once been such a big part of Brian's world. Knowing that his scholarship would continue to inspire music made my heart swell with both joy and sorrow.

At the luncheon, families shared emotional stories about their loved ones. I sat quietly, listening, reflecting, holding onto my own memories. Then, after lunch, the Jazz Band instructor approached me with a special invitation—would I like to hear a private saxophone performance by the quartet, featuring the scholarship recipient?

Of course, I would.

He led me into a small, intimate room and introduced me to the saxophonist. We shook hands, exchanged a few words, and then I took my seat. As the quartet began to play, I felt the music wash over me. But then, something happened that I can only describe as fate. The piece they chose wasn't just any song—it was one of Brian's all-time favorites: *When You Wish Upon a Star*.

The moment the first notes filled the air, I lost all composure. I sobbed the way I had when Brian died, overcome by the weight of love and loss. It was as if Brian himself had orchestrated this moment, whispering to me through the music, reminding me that he was still here, still with me. It was beautiful. Heartbreaking and healing all at once.

I don't believe in coincidences. Brian was a part of that moment— I know it with every fiber of my being. And as I left that day, I carried him with me, as I always do, tucked safely within my heart.

My mom, my three sisters, and Petey remain the cornerstone of my life. They hold the memories of who I was before meeting Brian, the happiness we shared, the journey through his illness, and the person I've become since his passing. They are my keepers of memory and my true home. My dad passed away 13 years ago. It's hard to believe so much time has passed. He was proud to see me moving forward, embracing a fuller life than before. For a long time, I resented his simple advice to "get a life," but I've come to understand that he said it because he wanted to see his daughter happy.

With Love,

Patty

www.ingramcontent.com/pod-product-compliance
Lightning Source LLC
Chambersburg PA
CBHW071237260626
47159CB00005BA/1760